May God Blast the Wom
Who Writes About Me

*Dios fulmine a la que
escriba sobre mí*

May God Blast the Woman
Who Writes About Me
*Dios fulmine a la que
escriba sobre mí*

a novel by
Aura García-Junco

translated by
Heather Cleary

—— MTO PRESS
WIVENHOE 2024

Contents

This book is for Juan, my brother

"*Perhaps this is what literature is, the invention of another life that could well be our own, the invention of a double.*"

— ENRIQUE VILA-MATAS, MONTANO'S MALADY
TR. JONATHAN DUNNE

"*though wish and world go down,
one poem yet shall swim*"

— E. E. CUMMINGS

"*and then came oblivion
to tell me almost in secret:
you won't see her again.
and with my eyes of a mute
with my lips of a blind man
I replied: who?*"

— H. PASCAL, NOCTURNE: GOODBYE

May God Blast the Woman
Who Writes About Me
*Dios fulmine a la que
escriba sobre mí*

PAPER BIRD

In the beginning was the word adorned with feathers: "The Jade-Green Bird," from a collection of Italian folk tales reimagined by Italo Calvino and read to me time and again by my father; the taciturn lamp, the little room with its red brick walls; his still-brown hair and the sound of his clear voice passing teeth, moustache, beard on each of the thousand and one nights of my childhood.

In the end was the word between the red covers of a book of poems that lay, shut like a tomb, on my father's belly when they found him dead. Between the terms "bird" and "earth" there is a thick forest of years during which distance consumed the complicity of my youth until I began to wonder if it had ever really existed, or if it had only been a dream from stories shared before bedtime.

My father loved beer but had habits that were, shall we say, less than refined. At restaurants he would order one and divide it between two glasses. Then he would dilute each half with water, most likely to save money. He did something similar with coffee. At La Blanquita, an americano with ice ("on the side please, Miss") was a discount frappe. Minor acts of culinary cupidity that bore no resemblance to the feasts he hosted at home. His preferred beverage at these was the shandy.

A shandy, according to my father: apple juice—the sweetest available, and lots of it—mixed with beer.

Archaeology of the shandy, according to my father: inspired by Vila-Matas.

Vila-Matas: "Shandy is commonly drunk in London—a mixture of beer and either fizzy lemonade or ginger beer—and a pint of shandy with ice is thirst-quenching in the summertime."

Obvious discrepancies with the quotation. I call it a *Goliardisation* of the beverage. Alfonso, my informant in this morbid endeavour of mine, counters that it is a *Pascalisation*. He is not talking about Blaise Pascal. My father baptised himself H. Pascal when he was a teenager, and that's what everyone called him. Everyone except his family. At home, he was Manuel. Juan Manuel.

*

I was the daughter who grimaced at his experiments with beer and turned crimson each time he shook his mullet and exclaimed "highway robbery!" when they brought the check in a restaurant. The little girl who never understood why she had to go to a technical high school instead of private school like her friends, just because he wanted to dedicate his life to literature.

(Why couldn't he be like my mother and get a steady job?) More recently, I was the woman who grappled with the worst aspects of his masculinity, the side of him that still weighs on me. And now I'm the woman who can't understand why her father ended up the way he did—alone with his books, sick and shut in. Unhappy.

At the same time, I was also the teenager who worshipped him secretly as part of a sect made up of goths like her. Because Pascal was also this: an eccentric force of nature, a planet that attracted countless people with his warmth and wisdom.

I was the daughter and now I don't know what I am.

*

For the past year, I have been living inside the grey of lingering secrets and lost embraces. A year of sadness masquerading as the mundane. I begin my research with the hope of delving into the closed book of his life so I can start a new chapter once this debt is paid. And, maybe, so I can learn to laugh with him, his unruly mullet bouncing triumphantly, at the miraculous multiplication of barley by which he turned one beer into two. Watery and foul, but two.

*

How can I get close to him? Memories are painful air. Whenever I try to grasp one, it slips through my fingers. All I have are the objects that he—unintentionally—left me.

*

For a long time, I thought my father would die with nothing. His patrimony consisted of the furnishings and books he was able to accumulate between four walls divided into two spaces: a living/dining room-office-library and a bedroom-library. It turns out that "nothing" feels quite voluminous when someone dies and those two rooms are, in fact, overflowing. A major problem for those left in the world, forced to stand in the middle of the material reality of what a father leaves behind. Read, in this case: my brother and me, working against the clock because the apartment was a rental and we needed to vacate it quickly. In two days, to be precise. Everything fits in the back of a junk dealer's pick-up if you pack it in right. And we packed it in right, between the garbage truck and the pick-up of a guy named Luis I found parked outside the Deportivo Miguel Alemán on that nightmarish Sunday when we needed to clean out my father's apartment.[1] We slid the rest—most of what was really the least—between the bars of our lives: half a jar of mayonnaise, a huge paella pan, his old Mac. His chapbooks. In the pages of one, Villaurrutia writes:

Death always takes the shape
of our bedroom.
It is concave and dark, silent and warm,
it gathers in the curtains where the shadows take shelter,

it is hard in the mirror and icy and tense,

---

1   CLEAN OUT: to eliminate all remaining traces of daily life.

deep in the pillows, white in the sheets.

I had never felt so intensely the way something intangible can fill a space with its warmth and its silence. And his sheets, the sadness of his pillows.

The belongings of someone who has died are kind of like props from a movie after filming ends. They sit in the limbo of having fulfilled their purpose. Decades before my brother and I opened the door to Juan Manuel's last apartment, Paul Auster stepped into the massive home where his father died. He writes, in *The Invention of Solitude*: "There is nothing more terrible, I learned, than having to face the objects of a dead man. Things are inert: they have meaning only in function of the life that makes use of them. When that life ends, the things change, even though they remain the same. They are there and yet not there: tangible ghosts, condemned to survive in a world they no longer belong to. What is one to think, for example, of a closetful of clothes waiting silently to be worn again by a man who will not be coming back to open the door?"

My brother and I, feigning more composure than we felt, opened our father's closet and, with our eyes fixed straight ahead, asked that same question. The clothing inside was in good condition. If we'd had more time or been more obsessive,[2] his clothes might have offered a chronology of his life. For example, a scarf from the period when he was a "serious" writer with a newspaper column on culture and the arts; a red jacket he must have worn when he had his radio program; and other items, stranger still, like a long velvet cape that dates, I

---

2   OBSESSIVE: How to free oneself from the rude pendulum that swings inside the mourning mind, that smashes back and forth with its ringing whenever we try not to think about the person who died?

think, to the many years he organised gothic festivals. Some people were surprised to learn that this extremely white fellow, with his mullet and his plaid shirts, would dedicate so much of his time to Mexico City's underground goth movement. I often heard him say that when it came to literature, goths were invisible to cultural institutions, but he believed they were the ones who most wanted to read: a whole urban subculture based on the adoration of art—or of a certain kind of art, at least. Thus began his self-inflicted mission to do something about it, which led to a whole series of eccentricities that started with goth culture but grew from there: heavy metal renditions of the poetry of Pablo Neruda in the Zócalo, rap based on Cortázar in the Insurgentes metro station, music inspired by Kafka at book fairs. These all raised more than a few conservative eyebrows. How dare some talc-dusted band sing verses of poetry to the sound of electric guitars? Who were all those tattooed types thronging the Museum of Mexico City one afternoon to see a performance based on so-and-so? Kids today! No respect for Literature.

My goth boots witnessed it all. So did the studs on my belt and my unbelievably painful septum piercing. By sixteen, I was already an expert at handing out flyers of questionable visual quality at the counterculture hub that was the Tianguis del Chopo and was going to El Circo Volador—a no-frills space for goth and metal shows where Bauhaus and PJ Harvey once played—almost every week. He always went with me, or rather I always went with him. But not even when a huge crowd from the *darks* scene withstood a torrential rainstorm out in the Zócalo to see (amazing) local bands pay homage to Neruda, did I see him wear the cape that appeared in his closet. That day, he was wearing a blue corduroy button-down over a t-shirt emblazoned with the logo of his life's work, the countercultural group Goliardos. As he weathered the down-pour like everyone else, he shouted to one of his students "Check it out! Tlaloc's a goth!" He was tenacious.

That t-shirt is draped across my lap as I write. There are pieces missing from its white logo, and the neck is all stretched out. It's so wide and short that it seems like it could only fit an overweight dwarf. My father, I should clarify, was not an over-weight dwarf, though in his later years—with snow whitening his thick eyebrows and carefully trimmed beard, with nicotine edging his fingers and moustache a deep yellow, with his five-foot-nine stature and the dark lashes and ironic glints of his small, piercing brown eyes—he did look a bit like a grunge-era Santa Claus. A year has gone by, and that stretched-out t-shirt still reeks of tobacco. Someone once told me she only had one item of clothing that smelled like her mother and that, racked with guilt after her mother's traumatic death, sinking her face into that sweater was her greatest source of comfort. One day, she came home to find the sweater in a pile of recently washed clothes. Time would eventually have robbed the sweater of her scent, but why so soon? Why like that? It was almost like losing her all over again.

I used to hate the smell of tobacco as much as I hated the addiction itself, but now I can't face the day when his things lose that scent. Luckily, paper doesn't get washed.

*

But the most important thing in my present investigation isn't this shirt—no matter how much I, too, insist on sniffing it from time to time. In front of me: two of the bookshelves made of reddish wood that crowned the hallway in the apart-ment where I spent my childhood. Two metres tall by one across. They might be described as "rustic," even though the boards are cut slim and appear to be of good quality. The difference: they're flat on their sides. Now they cover four meters of wall under my window. My parents had them made after they got married but he took them in the divorce, without discussion or permission. I'd say they have personality. If I were a little more out there, I'd even give them names. These new lodgers moved into my living room pregnant with volumes in July of 2019, at the end of the day when my brother and I stormed my father's apartment.

I don't fully understand what I have in front of me as I write, lying on my grey sofa, using a board as a desk. My rational side is inclined to interpret them as soulless objects; my penchant for magical thinking, to appreciate them as something else, something there are no words for. The physical, the physical. Cling to that. I don't want to dream, I don't want ethereal projections all over my living room. Be objects, blend in with the landscape; may the cats pee on you and may the plants shed their dead leaves and pests on you, and through this baptism of time may you be reborn clean and material, made of wood and nothing more.

*

For now, I tell myself: One step at a time. If you can't confront, imagine.

Imagine you have a bookshelf in front of you. Many volumes you always wanted to read are there. Expensive philosophical treatises you could never, would never have paid for. Antique volumes in German that attract you, even though you don't really know what they're about, and they endanger the books around them with the spores they contain. The complete works of several poets. Essays about literature and science. Latin American novels by the pound. Oddities long out of print. Signed editions of science fiction classics.

And yet, you don't dare touch it. You haven't in all this time. You've peeked at a couple of titles from the corner of your eye; people occasionally tell you what's there and sometimes even read snippets out loud. All you can do is stare at the shipwreck with a dead heart. Maybe this is why your first impulse, a year ago now, was to sell it. To free yourself as quickly as possible of this weight, like you and your brother did with the rest of his things. Then, as the months go by, you decide this is no way to live. You can't keep dragging a corpse around.

Stop imagining. The day has come.

You do finally dare, hand trembling and breath shallow, summoning all your courage, which is kind of absurd, you think, since what you are summoning your courage to do is, in fact, the trifle of taking a book from a shelf. You finally dare, I repeat, to take a book from the shelf. Strange: it's one you've owned, in another edition, for more than a decade. *Cosmicomics* by Italo Calvino. So why did you choose it? Maybe that was exactly why—to avoid immersing yourself in his personal library, to keep pretending you're in your own.

In any case, the spell is broken and the bookcase has let its guard down. You've shaken hands and now all that remains is to get familiar, to see if you can find among its dusty pages all those things left unsaid.

Dad: you left me a library and a mystery. In the presence of your thousands of books, surrounded by the ruins of what you had built, you took your last breath with a faint smile on your lips, as if sweet redemption awaited you just beyond the scythe. I never swear anything, but I swear this to you: I will try to understand you. I will invent you in order to give you the burial you never received. This is the beginning of nine months of mourning through words, through what you left behind. Marguerite Yourcenar said that one of the best ways to get to know someone is through their books. There must be some truth in that.

FIRST: THE DEAF ONE UNDERSTANDS THE SECRETS OF THE MOON

In the midst of a suspicious indolence disguised as professional obligations, I tell myself that since I already took the book off the shelf, I had better read it. Calvino accompanied me throughout the nights of my childhood, my wild adolescence, and the rare hours of my university life not absorbed by the classics department and its Ciceronian pull, so I take it as a good omen that I chose this duplicate text. At night, in this sad bed, I open my copy. Outside, the street is ablaze with ambulances.

*

As if to insist in the seriousness of this endeavour, I perform an act of bibliomancy and register the beginning of this exploration on a notecard:

Las cosmicómicas, Italo Calvino, Minotauro, 1985. Translated by Aurora Bernárdez. Net content: 12 atomic stories.

"I must add that past and future were vague terms for me, and I couldn't make much distinction between them: my memory didn't extend beyond the interminable present of our parallel fall, and what might have been before, since it couldn't be remembered, belonged to the same imaginary world as the future, and was confounded with the future."

---

*

Despite the initial rush, I'm not enjoying *Cosmicomics*. I'm not even really reading it. I had thought it would be easy, that I'd sit down and feel the same connection with the book I once felt. But it has kicked me out several times already. Maybe my sense of obligation to read and enjoy it won't let me past the first paragraph. I don't know. According to Vila-Matas in *Montano's Malady*, Robert Walser knew that writing about the impossibility of writing was also writing. I wonder if there's an equivalent for not-reading while one reads.

As I have failed to connect with the spiritual aspect of this book, having done little more than paw a greasy sheen across its covers, I will begin with material concerns.

Two books: mine and his. The yellowed pages of one give off the strange odour of tobacco. His edition turned thirty-six; it's the one from 1985. Mine, from 1999, is a fresh-faced twenty-two.

<u>1999</u>. Purchased in a used bookstore on calle Donceles when I was in high school. It cost—according to the pencilled marking on the first page—150 pesos. A fortune for me, back then. It was the successor to a copy I had loaned to someone.[3] My talisman-book needed to return to the floor I used back then as a dresser, beside the mattress that was my bed. It is my history, just as much as it is my book.

<u>1985</u>. On the fourth page, under the title, appears the long, pointy script my father would stab into his books: Juan Manuel García-Junco Machado 1985. A handwritten ex libris. Proof that this copy survived all the purges sparked by moves and financial woes.

<u>1999</u>. Greyish-blue cover.

<u>1985</u>. Oxford blue.

<u>1999</u>. White pages, good condition.

<u>1985</u>. Yellowed pages with brownish stain at the edge, appears to be grease.

---

3   TO LOAN A BOOK: Maybe the best way to give someone a present.

27

Both: ugly typeface on the cover and a line drawing of a dinosaur. The twenty-year-old sinks the grey image of the animal into the waters of its blue. The one in its thirties puts it front and centre among lines that simulate the cosmos. One point for 1985: the image is much nicer than the drowned dinosaur.

In 1985, Ediciones Minotauro recommended Ballard, Calvino, Carter, Phillip K. Dick, Schmidt, and Tolkien on the flap. An unparalleled selection.

By 1999, Ediciones Minotauro no longer made recommendations.

If my father died in 2019 and signed this book in 1985, then it lived with him for thirty-four years. I lived with him for just fourteen years and knew him for thirty. Another point for the book.

While I skip back and forth between the two editions, my soul crumples at the thought of how many books marked with that same signature, "Juan Manuel García-Junco Machado," were lost among the hundreds we threw out.[4] Now I can't rid myself of a single one—not even if I have nowhere to put them, not even if I don't read them. I am condemned to duplicate copies and enlightened junk. When someone is forced into the same horrific mission of sorting through my belongings—or, rather, the belongings of a corpse—maybe they'll find themselves in the same quandary, but this time tripled: their own *Cosmicomics* and mine and also the copy belonging to my father, whose name will have become a mere echo of the past. I hope my future cats are big readers because

---

4   SOUL: In the most literal sense, I believe that my soul lives in the pit of my stomach. I'm not saying anyone else's soul is located there, necessarily, but mine is. The proof: that metaphysical wrenching when my anxiety about something causes me pain could only come from my soul.

the way things are going, they'll be my sole heirs. I also hope that my future cats are financially solvent and have their papers in order so they can rent an apartment big enough to house their life plus an inheritance, which is to say someone else's life.

But I digress. I digress to avoid reading, and I avoid reading because I'm afraid of understanding.

*

Two photos, tucked among the pages:

1) A man in his thirties. Handsome. Thick brown hair, heavy brows over small eyes. Thick-rimmed glasses, always. A grey wool blazer with elbow patches. Jeans. The launch of one of his novels published by a "respectable" house?[5] White teeth showing in a faintly mocking smile.

2) A red-faced man, swollen, with a tousled mullet. Greasy hair, impeccable beard. A threadbare but clean button-down. Faded black trousers with whitish stains, possibly talcum powder. Missing teeth. Crocs: atrocious, but necessary for feet bursting with water. A sad smile. Blurred photo.

The cliché of comparing these pictures smacks me in the face while the reality of their contents insists on proving that sometimes a thing repeated many times can still transmit a profound truth.

If the first photo were a movie, the protagonist and his wife would return home, where a little girl and a little boy would be waiting in their beds. She is ten; he is six. His strong arms could carry them both at once; his sturdy legs, run miles and miles to reach them; with his brio, he could read and read

---

5   RESPECTABLE PUBLISHING HOUSE: Another way of saying we have no idea what respect is.

and write and write without pause. Demand publication and get it. Organise unlikely festivals and pay for them hell or high water. Call mythical authors and promising young writers and speak to them in English, despite not speaking English, to get them to Mexico.

If the second photo were a movie, the man would return to his apartment building after teaching a workshop and would laboriously climb the stairs. His knee would emit sharp bursts of pain while the rest of his body demanded immediate relief for his bladder. Surrounded by his yellowed walls and the dust of his books, he would receive calls from his son and his mother, to whom he would complain about how long he's been out of work. These conversations would be sweet, loving and would bring a smile to his face. He would ask his son for a loan to pay his rent and then, after hanging up, he'd begin his endless scrolling through social media, that hellish loop. He would try to write and fail, try to read and find his attempts thwarted by a shapeless disquiet. He'd call his daughter, who would be thirty by this time; she'd see his number and decide not to answer. He would send links and post on his wall until late. Take a sleeping pill and set out along the cruel road of his nightly insomnia.

Between the blurred scenes of these two photos: assorted joys, evanescent flames. Dazzling blazes. Years.

*

The question—the maddening ouroboros of my days—is: Why? The man whose cultural project reached thousands. The man some called Sensei with a mixture of irony and absolute sincerity. The man who wrote novels and even published one with a legendary genre fiction house in Spain when no one else was doing anything of the sort. What came between these two photos?

A writer who stopped writing because he "just couldn't anymore." Blocked and in bad health; bitter on many fronts, loving on others.

When did his life force start dripping from his veins to eat through everything around him?

Why?

The question, which was the stuff of my nightmares when he was still alive, is now a mystery I can't bring myself to label banal. It turns out that death isn't offering me the perspective I'd hoped for, and that I'm just as tortured by his secrets as I am by my own.

I walk the four metres of his bookshelves, letting my fingertips brush against the spines of all those books; I repeat, return, touch, close my eyes, lose my mind, and all the while I can only ask: Why?

*

I drag a white armchair across the floor, a coffee table. A cat chase makes room for the furniture to pass. The furniture, for its part, makes room for the bookshelves. Whenever I move, the first thing I think about is where the hell I'm going to put all these boxes of books.

A few months ago, as I considered my life as the Newly Appointed Owner of an Untouchable Library, it occurred to me that I should probably say something about it. I wanted to write an exquisite treatise on the spiritual depth of the personal library, those spaces that contain, between leather-bound covers, all the greatness of Mankind. About how it's not opposable thumbs or walking upright or advanced cognition that makes us human but rather a particular way of looking at the world through the prism of words. About how books might not make us better, but they do invite us to engage with other voices. And yet, despite what my choice of careers might suggest, I'm a practical person and it wasn't long before I realised that, in these times of dispossession, a personal library is, above all, a pain in the ass.

Each time I buy a book, I imagine the eventuality of a move. Its three-dimensional presence, an innocent 880 grams on average, becomes a large-scale affront when joined by an army of its peers. Given, of course, that your apartment is never your own and you have to move over and over again.

In part from the fear that grows more intense as each lease renewal approaches, and in part due to the number of volumes that mysteriously accumulated on the most unlikely surfaces (I'll never forget the small pile that began to eat away at my bed), I decided a few years ago to stop buying books. In a minimalist rapture perhaps inspired by Marie Kondo's sudden fame, I pulled from my shelves books I had already read or would never read and told myself I would sell them. I even made a list in Excel, like a real adult, and priced them according to a combination of speculation and intuition. But I am a good, upstanding woman, so first things first: I sent the list to my father to see if he wanted back any of the books that had come from him. Many had been a loan, a gift, or something on the hazy border in between. Some had been in my possession for more than a decade but were still his, nonetheless. He wanted all of them back—even the ones he had surely forgotten about, even the ones he had no room for in his overflowing lair. I set them aside in a box.

O, apathy: with the Excel and everything, I didn't sell a single volume and the box of books remained right there, next to the couch. Then there was no one to return them to. When my father's two enormous bookshelves appeared in my apartment, that was the end of line for those Itinerant Loaners, which returned to their Ithaca after being shipwrecked in each of my many homes over the course of ten years. Books are my shadow. Even when I try to get rid of one, it comes back to me by some convoluted path. I'll die drowning in them, just like he did.

As we emptied my father's apartment in fast forward, physical reality imposed itself in all its fury: each additional cubic metre in my apartment would have meant 50 or so books saved from the junk dealer. A space that was truly mine—assured by title and certificate, freed from the burden of future moves—was the destiny I would have needed in order to bring with me all the parts of him we threw away in those yellowed pages.

But that doesn't really matter right now, because I haven't been able to read the books I did manage to bring home. I content myself with staring at the bookshelves, hypnotised, my gaze empty and dry. And in this involuntary meditation, I remember things.

*

I remember. How on each of my sporadic visits, his house brimmed with the smells of the most heterodox foods: beer in dishes that didn't call for it, vegetables that were never meant to go together (but which tasted surprisingly good), medieval stews meant to settle the stomach. Combinations born of imagination like stories improvised during a night of insomnia. There was always far more food than we could eat, and by the end my green shopping bags, the "earth-friendly"

33

kind (another gift), would be filled not only with books but also with a cornucopia of a kilo or two of strawberries, a plastic container of stew, single-serving packets of tuna and who knows what else. I remember arriving home and removing one book after another, scratching my head over where on earth I was going to put them, my space always on the verge of overflowing.

*

I remember. Once, many years ago, H. Pascal tried to bring Ray Bradbury to Mexico for a science fiction festival. My witnesses attest to having heard him call the legend from a back room in my aunt's house, his headquarters at the time. Bradbury was old and confined to a wheelchair. The negotiation was with his wife.

It's hard for me to imagine my father making that call with his broken English. It's not hard for me to imagine H. Pascal doing it. This isn't the only time I saw him commit acts of daring that went far beyond the limits of decorum. Another: when I was a little girl, Pascal was invited to participate in the Semana Negra de Gijón, a literary festival dedicated to genre fiction. As was always the case, he couldn't afford to go, so he set out on a mission that was bound to fail. He called Aeroméxico and offered an exchange: a ticket to Spain for ad space in his publication.

And by publication he meant:

Goliardos, his life's work, which lasted so long and required so much effort that it became his identity. A publishing house for "marginal" genres like science fiction, horror and crime fiction. Most editions were stapled fanzines with covers designed by Pascal himself that defied all aesthetic sensibility with their collaged images of nude vampires and asteroids. Victorian cyberpunk in black and white. Small print runs, obviously. In those days, the books sold out quickly and were constantly being reprinted. But part of the project was that they needed to be inexpensive so anyone could buy them. Hence lots of sales but little money. (Until it wasn't so little anymore, but that would come later.)

As I eavesdropped on his conversation with the representative from Aeroméxico, I wondered how he could believe a huge corporation would give him a ticket for publicity in a kitschy zine that got passed around among young people who rarely had a cent to their names. I felt ashamed, just like I did so many other times I heard him try to raise funds to keep Goliardos afloat in the face of all kinds of adversity and, especially, debts.

It was probably by taking on debt that he finally managed to buy that ticket.

Bradbury almost came to the festival. It was only his bad health that got in the way. Even so, when I heard the story, it was hard not to count it as a failure.

*

Sitting on the floor with my feet getting colder by the minute. I look at the shelves and their books and find them beautiful. I take pictures of them, run my fingers over old spines, new ones, the plastic still on several. A few of them force me to open them in search of their contents: my father had a habit of wrapping the covers of his most-used books.[6]

---

6   TO USE A BOOK: To wring its entrails until its juices are absorbed through your skin.

It's as if his final breath, that Rubicon of non-life, were dusted across those shelves in a fine layer, and I, desperate to hang on to my father, were greeting him every day when I look at them. Good morning, vast nothing. Good morning, eternal emptiness.

"Is that why it hurts me so much to have left dozens of books with the junk dealer?" I ask the deaf bookseller who is now my substitute father. Like in the first story of *Cosmicomics*, "The Distance of the Moon," his figure recedes from me and becomes in itself the question of how to reach it.

*

Insomnia. Guilt over my lack of progress. My father always said, half-quoting Charles Chaplin, that life is a desire, not a meaning. But what happens when we stop desiring? It's past midnight. Without looking at the story, I recite "The Distance of the Moon" and wrap my arms around myself.

*

I tried to forge ahead in the safety of the daylight that floods my third-floor apartment in waves, filling it with a sweaty, peaceful heat. The result: 1) hours of scrolling through social media; 2) cleaning my entire house, even those hidden corners that could have perfectly well gone on collecting dirt. Then my procrastination takes a mysterious turn and, in order to avoid reading, I begin researching Calvino. *Cosmicomics* belongs to what some critics call his "late" period, which is less exciting than it sounds: they mean the works published between the appearance of *Cosmicomics* in 1965 and the author's death in 1985. This period coincides with his time in Paris, when he was invited to join Oulipo (Workshop of Potential Literature). Many critics agree: this is his crappiest period. Imagine that you have a prolific career, that you've written numerous books and these have moved countless people for decades, that you're respected and have managed to make a living from that juggling act called writing, and after all that a bunch of critics state categorically that the work you made during the last twenty years of your life is your worst. Just imagine.

The members of Oulipo established (establish, the group still exists) sets of rules for writing their texts. Calvino, who had always been interested in science, gladly joined the ranks of a collective driven by the dialectic between literature and theory, that unusual catalyst. Each story in *Cosmicomics* takes physics as its point of departure, from the rotation of the planets to the origins of colour. Curiously, many of the theories have been discarded but the stories remain.

*

I guess my father, like so many writers, held some vague ambition to become eternal, to exist beyond the scientific theories that watched him grow. To conquer science with art. To conquer biochemistry with the metaphysics of creation. A pretty thankless desire, if you ask me. So what happened? Why stop writing? Why use the finite hours in the day to talk about other people's work? Sometimes I think, because I feel it in me, that the blighted career we call writing could very well, and very easily, break a person. But it needs an extra something in order to do that: a gaping wound awaiting an infection.

*

I've always felt an affinity with Oulipo. Aside from the small detail that women weren't exactly regulars among its numbers over the years, sometimes I think I would be a respectable recruit. Right now, for example, I'm weaving my grief with the thread of these books. Turning an object into structure and meaning.

*

Maybe this explains my pride when I look at my personal library, even though it's not an accomplishment in itself. I wish I could kill my fetish for books and all the biases that go along with it. But my idea of home is so tied to them that the dust between their pages is the seasoning sprinkled over my apartments, and the books themselves are my sustenance. When I was little, my classmates always felt strange as they stepped into our 70 square metre apartment, which was more paper than people. Lining a hallway so narrow you couldn't open your arms all the way, our bookshelves stretched from the floor to the ceiling. That was our home and our day-to-day, as if piles of books were a special colour of paint for the walls. My mother contributed a bunch of psychology books and a few more of literature. My father, his eclectic excess. Sometimes there wasn't enough money to pay for anything, but there was always a book for everything: from encyclopaedias of human sexuality to pulp horror. I never considered this a personal library. For me, it had no name. It just was.

*

Even now, my definition of a library comes from two places. If I close my eyes, the first thing that appears are dark wooden bookshelves lining walls at least four metres high, curtains as dusty as they are thick, tomes bound in dark leather that no one could lift with one hand. Victorian opulence. Between the mahogany and a fireplace, I see myself standing next to Jane Eyre in the library where she will give classes to Adèle, the master's illegitimate daughter. "Most of the books were locked up behind glass doors ... In this room, too, there was a cabinet piano, quite new and of superior tone; also an easel for painting and a pair of globes." Private libraries in impossible homes, in all their bourgeois abundance and excess. I don't fully understand how the gothic inserted itself so definitively in my brain.

In diametrical opposition to this image, a list of the real libraries in my life comes to mind: the rickety bookshelves at Secundaria Técnica 32. The library at Prepa 9—awful, gloomy. The beautiful Biblioteca Central, with its grey steel shelves and overwhelming rooms where the only drive stronger than sleep was my fear someone might catch me dozing. The Samuel Ramos, at UNAM's Facultad de Filosofía y Letras, where I learned the true meaning of neurosis whenever the students from the library studies program gathered outside their classroom door, talking without any consideration for the budding philologists trying to memorise Julius Caesar before our next Latin class. Weekends at the Biblioteca Vasconcelos, sitting next to a homeless person at rest on those brightly coloured chairs, staring up at the hollows inside Gabriel Orozco's whale.

The library in my fantasies was opulent, impossible. The ones in my reality were public. The one in my house wasn't a library. Several cats in a room can be several cats in a room, or they can be a pack. Ten yellow apples in a basket on the dining room table can be apples, or they can be "fruit." Five stamps can be a collection, or they can just be five stamps. I learned that the term "library" could be applied to one's own books when someone I was studying with at the university died and the department coordinator mentioned that his parents were going to donate his "personal library" to the school. Since then, the idea of the personal library has been connected in my mind to the idea of death. Maybe one's assortment of books only becomes a library in someone else's eyes. The good news is that their accumulation is finite and will eventually end. The bad news is that those of us with this fetish can't find an obstacle powerful enough, except death, to keep us from buying more books.

"The perfect order is impossible," says Roberto Calasso, "due to the existence of entropy. But one cannot live without order. With books, as with all else, one must find a middle ground between these two statements." This middle ground was completely absent from my house. Accumulation. The joint collection of my father, my mother, and later mine and my brother's was only that: books. An object at once so common and so revered it ended up endowed with a mystical quality that its contents often didn't merit.

This disorder—the dearth of classification or the surplus of entropy (read: chaos)—is why the books in my childhood home were never a library or a pack but only an expansive mess, necessary decoration, refuge or grievance, depending on the day.

Now my living room holds books that explicitly comprise a "library," that is, the ones I inherited. In this movement from one hand to another, from a dead man to a living woman, they became a set, and I have no choice but to reimagine my definition of a library, though it feels a bit pompous to apply this term to the unkempt bookcases that are the backdrop of my hungover mornings, my most stressful meetings, and my sweaty home exercise sessions. They don't quite seem to fit the definition. My shelves hold not only books, but also little cat alebrijes and renegade mugs forgotten until the green tea they once held dries and stains the ceramic. My bookshelf is a closer relative to a threadbare couch than to Alexandria. Jane Eyre's ghost isn't wandering around, eyeing their spines; no one is looking up their titles in an orderly catalogue and, frankly, it's hard to find one if you do look for it. Long live entropic, chaotic, dishevelled personal libraries.

*

Today I'm not even going to try. I spent the morning going over our correspondence on social media.

At 5:19am on July 2, 2019, my father sent a link.

Very interesting. To listen and read. With subtitles and bilingual text…

The website contained three poems by Mary Jo Bang. When I woke up that morning, I saw his message and felt a familiar pain.[7] Awake again in the middle of the night? The return of the insomnia that had attacked him so viciously for years?

My father sent links to poems, cultural events and events

---

7   THE PAIN: The Pain that erupts at the most unexpected moments, as a visit from the ghost of memory, feels surprisingly similar each time—like a downward tug from my esophagus to my stomach, like a hand scraping an object along my connective tissue, pulling on my throat as it passes. A strange kind of heartburn accompanies this sensation that only rarely leads to tears.

in line with his project all the time. I'd gotten used to ignoring them. At first, I wasn't sure if he was only sending them to me, but then a few of my friends (mostly women writers, but also a guy or two), told me that they got them, too. Was he that lonely? Did it annoy my friends, even though they claimed it didn't? Above all, I didn't want anyone thinking about him like I did, with the same anger and rejection.

The calendar says it was a Tuesday. I didn't click the link or send a reply. I got to work, trying desperately to quiet the questions nagging at me, stirring the insides of my chest.

The next message in that conversation simply reads: "Are you okay?" I sent it at 11:30am that same day, after my uncle called me to say that the cleaning woman (whose services he paid for) had found my father lying down. That he wasn't breathing. "I've rejected the milk-mild/smile. It's married to the risk of fossilization," writes Mary Jo Bang in her poem, "The Mirror."

I've rejected the milk-mild
smile. It's married to the risk of fossilization.
Granite with blood in its veins is still granite.
On the bark of the pine behind me, a single
cicada is glittering. That world is an island
where it is always morning and the cool
breeze is always invigorating. You can tell
by my hair, how it's blown back. You can
tell by the light. It's there and not going
anywhere. There is no moment that isn't all
spectacle. The theatrical silence is the sun.
The grey stage is winter. The circle is pure
dilation: the shock mouth of me looking back
at an avalanche of broken glass.

A poem as life itself, beginning with blood—but in granite—
and ending with a smile that is an avalanche of broken glass. I
hadn't read it until today. I really liked it.

*

The cover of my father's *Cosmicomics* looms over me. From
a distance, I look at it like one of the cats that live with me
when it's stalking the other. There it is, a pulsing threat, on
the arm of the couch. It's just an object, I repeat to myself.
My mother sends me a text message to ask how I'm doing.
Fine, I write. One word. I set my phone aside and take a deep
breath to crawl, with feline movements, over to the couch.
There's something in the impossibility of reading, in Mary Jo
Bang's poems, in the messages posted on my wall that sinks
me into something like dense water, like the Black Sea, where
nothingness dwells. My right hand shakes. The Pain makes its
presence felt.

   Then comes the cruel interference. A series of images that
appear before me in the blink of an eye: my father, who is
no longer my father, in a coffin, silent for the first time. The
black dress I wore, my brother nearby. My mother, who in all
these years never let him fall, despite everything. The obligation to smile at people as they arrived, to be a kind of hostess
in the worst moment of my life. The sensation of failing at that.
The indecision: if I laugh right now is it an insult or what he
would have wanted, given his dark sense of humour? How am
I supposed to behave at my father's funeral? There should be
some kind of instruction manual for this inevitable occasion,
I think. (But who would want to read it?) My uncle, who was
also always there for him, who always said my father was like
his own, couldn't go. His brother and sister, unable to cry.

My grandmother, who finally arrives and collapses before the inert figure of her second child. A tearing out of insides. Pure unreality. People dressed in black arrive who didn't know him but did admire him; writers arrive who were sometimes his friends and other times not so much. Musicians and singers who played bizarre versions of poems at his events. His students arrive. People arrive who will hold me for the rest of my life just because they were there on the only day it was truly necessary. And you think to yourself that, amid all this love, you can survive this.

It's too late when you realise that this moment is only the first of many, day zero in an infection that spreads incessantly through your veins, your organs, every muscle of your body. That later, once the spell of having people around you has faded, what's left is an immense solitude. The worst of all deserts.

*

But it has been—I count them—thirteen months since then. Why do I still feel the same wrenching sensation when I remember my grandmother with her wrinkled cheeks, held up by her son on the left and her daughter on the right, crumpled over the cold glass that separated her from my father? Why does The Pain still assault me between one sentence and another?

Shouldn't I be able to do something as basic as what I'm proposing here?

*

Maybe I'm taking this too personally.[8] Maybe if I read more, if I zoom out, everything will be easier. Think more about the stories and less about myself. *Cosmicomics* belongs to a tradition that describes formations of the universe, mythical cosmogonies. It jumps to the moon and then back to the sea, always anchored in the reveries of fictional speculation.

Calvino wrote a book in which every aspect of being here, of being a living part of a planet slow cooked over centuries, feels like a mystery worth exploring. I look at my bookshelves and the string lights shaped like stars that since yesterday have been making a bright zigzag across them, and I think about how they're made of molecules and atoms. That's the extent of my science, but not of my imagination. The physical matter remains.

The string lights look good on them: it's like putting a collar on a cat, in part so it doesn't get lost, and in part to declare that it belongs to you and no one else.

*

I pick up *The Invention of Solitude*, that classic about a father's death and am knocked back by how swiftly Paul Auster sums up a life, his father's life, in sharp, confident adjectives:

> For fifteen years he had lived alone. Doggedly, opaquely, as if immune to the world … an emotional lethargy that prevented him from taking any action.

---

8   PERSONALLY: Thinking about a book is personal. Saying what I think about certain texts feels like stripping naked in public.

45

In *The Situation and the Story*, Vivian Gornick states that in order to write personal fiction, the author must be able to distance him or herself from the story enough to gain the reader's trust. There's so much artifice in writing, even when writing about one's own life. When I read Auster, I feel the proximity of the event—his grief unfolds before my eyes. That book was written just a few months after his father's death. I think I understand what Gornick was saying, because his machete judgements hurt my eyes; all the rage and sadness tell me more about his grief than about the individual to whom they refer. Even so, I'm not sure there's another way.

As an example of the ideal distance, Gornick recounts that J. R. Ackerley, author of a memoir titled *My Father and Myself* (cough, cough). It took Ackerley thirty years to find the right narrative voice for his story. Thirty years to achieve the right level of detachment. Thirty years to become a narrator able to gain the reader's trust. Gornick describes his process: "After another while he realized, I always thought my father didn't want to know me. Now I see I didn't want to know him. And then he realized, it's not him I haven't wanted to know, it's myself."

Condensed in these words are the conclusions of thirty years of self-examination and, certainly, of obsession with a story. I don't want to finally want to write this book after thirty years of having a ghost ramble around in my head. I don't want to spend thirty years savouring that particular brand of madness.

Gornick says it's possible to have the situation (the life to narrate, for example) but not the story. When I sit down to write, I'm missing both. I had planned to research my father, to write about the smile on his face when he died and, most of all, about his life, without ever asking myself where I fit into that narrative. The paradox is that I realise I never wanted to know him, not really. Ackerley's three statements—the cyclical movement between them—seem to contradict themselves at every turn; even if I don't understand that movement, I do feel it. That cycle between not wanting to know anything and wanting to know everything; between wanting to forget and wanting to remember things you never knew. That pulsing question: Why?

*

2008:
More than 70 titles published, twice awarded the National Prize for Fantastic Literature, over 15 concerts in Mexico City's Zócalo, where, thanks to these shows (and to the best groups in the Mexican gothic movement, and to all of you who filled the Zócalo with shadows every time) the goth scene made its way into the broader world in the most important public space in the nation, the magical centre of the continent.
(Goliardos website.)

2018:
Luck hasn't changed,
it is seen from afar
or from too close:
the fate is the same.
("Proof of Existence," H. Pascal)

Why?

*

I open the book at random. Story number ten: "The Form of Space," an endless descent through, well, space, during which the unnamed narrator (Qfwfq?) dreams of being able to touch Ursula H'x, a beautiful woman. Impossible: the form of space demands that their trajectories will remain strictly parallel.

I don't remember a single word of it. I've spent decades insisting that *Cosmicomics* was the book I read most often as a teenager. Now I think about it and, though it might be early for confessions, here I go: I'm no longer sure I ever read the whole thing. I'm beginning to understand those mythomaniacs who claim not to know which of their accounts are lies. My memory is a disgrace. How can I figure this out? As a teenager, I was primarily concerned with making out. I did it well, in the afternoons and the mornings before high school, on dirty park benches and along the horrific Avenida Insurgentes. It's hard to read with all those hormones flowing. What isn't hard is following the script of what you think you're supposed to be: I was the goth girl who read. By then, I had already figured out that the occupation "writer" wasn't just uncommon in my social circles, it was almost like saying "astronaut." Being the daughter of a writer and a psychologist guaranteed I'd be labelled as weird, and I wore it like a badge of honour—even if I didn't back it up by reading all the time. I read little and badly, but no one caught on. I, too, was a fraud.

For now, whether I've read it a thousand times or none, my skill with literary analysis is sufficient to assert the following: it takes serious balls to name your protagonist Qfwfq. All the names in this book seem to demand reading in silence. They ask to be thought of as images on the page rather than words leaving a mouth. Stories of extraordinary beauty that are a nightmare to read aloud.

*

Other notable names in *Cosmicomics*:
- Captain Vhd Vhd
- Kgwkg
- (k)yK
- N'ba N'ga
- Mr. Pbert Pberd

*

I underlined his book. With a pencil, and after much vacillation. The almost invisible rasp of the porous yellow page made me click my tongue. I don't know if this book can go back to its old shelf, not after being profaned.

*

A library is more than the sum of its works. I'm not sure what it transmits about its owner beyond a penchant, which sometimes borders on the pathological, for accumulating dusty volumes, many of which she will never read. My father's had an unusual number of duplicates. Perhaps the most striking manifestations of his unhealthy addiction were the entire collections he would buy on sale at used bookstores, or editions put out by the ministry of culture that ended up in boxes. It wasn't unusual for him to give someone the same book two or even three times. Or to give copies of the same title to different people for Christmas. He was a mass gifter of books. Many were lost in the Great Post Mortem Purge, but a few clones remain and I will eventually give them away, fulfilling their destiny.

*

Magic. With my feet on the coffee table and the smell of black tea wafting around me, I am enjoying *Cosmicomics*. I enter the stories slowly and live within their figures. Giving up the idea that I need to love the book because I loved it in the past was the key to reading it with pleasure. Now I play with it, rewrite it, adopt it, and it finds its way into my dreams.

As I read, I follow an invisible thread. I search for the golden fleece: the strength to connect the book in my hands to my father, not through my experience of the book, but through the words it contains. I turn my *Cosmicomics* into the I Ching. We all know there's no such thing as objectivity, but the way I wallow in these stories, seeing only what I want to, really takes the cake. This outrageous space is the opposite of what turned Quixote into a knight: he introduced literary fantasy into his reality, whereas I want to wedge my life in among the pages.

For example, Calvino writes: "Let me make one thing clear: this theory that the universe will condense again after reaching an extremity of rarefaction [and we'll be reunited at that point to start over] has never convinced me." I can't be the only one who sees in these lines the promise of life after death, a place where the dead and the living are reunited "to start over." Like Mr. Qfwfq, I've never found the idea very convincing.

*

In the same story, "All At One Point," Calvino runs into an old friend and they talk about Mrs. Ph(i)Nk0—"her bosom, her thighs"—the only woman from that distant time whom no one has forgotten. The one who provoked neither jealousy nor gossip among the men. Because they all occupy a single point in space, given that the universe hasn't yet expanded, the good lady sleeps with all of them at once. And the narrator muses, "what more could I ask?"

He could ask, for example, for a dinner to accompany this delight, which is precisely what the good Mrs. Ph(i)Nk0 offers immediately thereafter. Noodles for all! If only she had some room… This act of love is the catalyst by which matter begins to expand in the universe. Big bang! Next comes a sumptuous series of phrases about the creation of the universe:

> and at the same time we thought of it, this space was inevitably being formed, at the same time that Mrs. Ph(i)Nk0 was uttering those words: ". . . ah, what noodles, boys!" the point that contained her and all of us was expanding…

Creation ex nihilo, the neatness of a birth without blood or shit. Calvino's writing, asserts Kathryn Hume, withdraws from the sensual. I agree: it's cold, like a polished crystal that refracts in all directions. There is no sweat beading on skin, no unpleasant odours. There is hypnosis, but no seduction.

I feel like I'm watching a beautiful event unfold through a store window.

*

Though I can read "All at One Point" and sense the imaginative pleasure Calvino took in turning a plain theory of physics into an unexpected story, as he did in so many books, interference cuts through this pleasure. I can't help but see in Mrs. Ph(i) Nk0 the perfect male fantasy: a woman who cooks, is sexual but modest, and always entirely generous. Often when I notice those things not explicitly said, like the eloquent celebration of a bosom and thighs as the first (and most important) characteristics of a female character, I feel like a killjoy. To be clear: I feel like me, at my own birthday party, stomping my own tres leches cake while another part of me runs over to try and stop me.

Sara Ahmed talks about the figure of the unhappy feminist: "To be against forms of power and violence that are concealed under signs of happiness does not necessarily mean becoming unhappy, even if it does mean refusing to go along with things by showing signs of getting along." I agree and wouldn't call myself unhappy, just occasionally nostalgic. At those moments, I long for the time when "All at One Point" was simply a myth about matter expanding in the universe framed as a love story. I often get bored of the cables in my head that won't let me read another way anymore. It's hard to come to terms with that loss of innocence, especially when I return to books I read a long time ago and loved (or love) deeply, and even more so when those books were written before these debates were widespread.

The same thing happens when I return to experiences and people from my past. What had been an uncomfortable flirtation becomes harassment under the magnifying lens of time, and what had been my father introducing me to his young girlfriend becomes a real headache. (Okay, who am I kidding? It was always that.) The malicious alchemy of time and of ideological change. But I won't get into that here. Not yet.

*

If I spilled a drop of beer on his copy, is it truly mine now? If I read it a little bit tipsy, does that make it even more mine? I finished the book tonight and felt an emptiness that's actually an invitation to read. The problem with emptiness is that it also opens space for lingering questions.

SECOND: FEMME FATALE FILING HER NAILS

Unlike Calvino, my father was not crystal but flesh. I find a quotation from Lorenz Okenfuss in one of his novels that is the reverse image of "All at One Point":

> The movement of astral bodies anticipates the supreme act of animal life, which is copulation. Creation itself is none other than the act of fertilization. From the very beginning, sex has been present as a sacred bond that keeps nature whole. Those who deny sex fail to understand the mystery of the universe.

H. Pascal wrote poetry and fiction, often erotica. One uncle still enjoys bringing up one of his early novels, *Las anémonas*, named after the flower, and referring to it as pornography. Its description on Goodreads:

> Pre-Islamic Arabia: magic, conspiracies, sexuality at its most extreme. The legendary kingdom of Hita: political intrigue, erotic dark magic, ambition and power set against desire. *Las anémonas*, a garden where love and murder create ghosts, torments, indelible stigmata...

Historical erotic fantasy, his specialty. I don't have a copy of that specific title, but I do have several others, which I flip through from time to time, not daring to actually read them. I weigh the pros and cons. I mean, it might be a necessary part of this research, but it might also force me to gouge out my own eyes. I'm not sure it would be worth it, this sacrifice in the name of art.

*

Another act of divination and chance sends my hands toward the bookshelf on the left. As if by design, I find myself facing an author I've been thinking about a lot these days due to our shared love of writing about literature and its makers: Enrique Vila-Matas.

Historia abreviada de la literatura portátil, Enrique Vila-Matas, Anagrama, 2014. Net contents: a brief history of portable literature.

"The portable writers always behaved like irresponsible children. From the outset, they established staying single as an essential requirement for entering into the Shandy secret society or, at least, acting as though one were."

That was how, without meaning to, I returned to one of my teenage favourites, one of the bonds I shared with my father. We didn't talk much about Vila-Matas, but we knew he was something we had in common. Actually, we didn't talk about any book. My father would lecture at me like he did with his female students, the only difference being that I was an unreceptive audience in a state of constant rebellion against his professorial persona. Sometimes, when he was in a good mood and I mentioned some book or another, he would beam with the kind of smile only food and literature ignited in him. For years, Vila-Matas was our spark plug.

I don't know what I am, but it's clear to me that my father was literature-sick. "I am literature-sick. If I carry on like this, literature could end up swallowing me," says the narrator of *Montano's Malady*, one of my favourite novels not to read when

I was in my twenties.[9] It makes me think of all the texts my father knew by memory. He was a walking encyclopaedia who could recite thousands of poems and then immediately let out a loud, shameless burp.

Top that, Montano.

*

A Brief History of Portable Literature is still one of my favourite books. In it, Vila-Matas talks about shandies. In addition to being a drink that, no matter how much my father insisted, did not consist of apple juice and beer, the term also referred in parts of Yorkshire to someone who was "joyful as well as voluble or zany." Hence the name of the eccentric protagonist of another adored book, *The Life and Opinions of Tristram Shandy, Gentleman.*

The narrator-researcher traces the history of the Shandy secret society, that wild imaginary entity that consolidated a group of artists according to a clearly defined set of characteristics: being bachelor machines, having a body of work that could fit in a suitcase, a disinterest in grand statements, madness tending toward suicide (and then not), a fraught coexistence with doppelgängers and a sympathy for negritude (???). Vila-Matas weaves together history and invention, and throws characters like Marcel Duchamp, Francis Picabia, Tristan Tzara, Georgia O'Keeffe, Salvador Dalí, Man Ray, Ezra Pound, Juan Gris, Scott Fitzgerald and Max Ernst together in a

---

9   FAVOURITE NOVELS NOT TO READ: The idea behind these novels is so seductive that they can be counted as favourites whether or not you've read them.

single sack. Ridiculous anecdotes, unexpected sequences, and so, so much well-executed name-dropping.

What a beautiful trip, inhabiting this imaginary period in the Catalan writer's company.

*

Portable literature is, well, portable. The members of the Shandy secret society are, or believe themselves to be, proponents of a certain lightness. Their work has no room, at least discursively, for grand statements. Oh, the delightful delusion that we don't want much. It reminds me of the point when my father declared himself a key player on Team Dispossessed. And while there's certainly some truth there (speculative fiction has always been marginalised), there's also something peremptory and dishonest about announcing a disinterest in grand statements. I'm sure that at the beginning of his career, with his first novels brimming with pages and extensive research, my father's literature wasn't portable. That when the literary establishment put him in his place,[10] telling him that you can't be a serious novelist if all you write is science fiction or unhinged erotica, he let out a proud and hushed "I didn't want that, anyway" and decided to follow another path. I might have done the same thing. But I also know that whenever you act without introspection, without recognising pain or daring to express it, bitterness takes root somewhere in your chest and it never leaves. And, little by little, you end up fighting with everyone.

However it happened, at a certain point my father's

---

10   TO PUT SOMEONE IN THEIR PLACE: Those who think in these terms forget that we all occupied the same point in space before the Big Bang.

literature most certainly became portable. I couldn't imagine a better recruit for the Shandys than Goliardos. The project meets all the requirements: "cultivation of the art of insolence, and passion for traveling with a small suitcase containing almost weightless versions of his work," bachelor machines, extreme sexuality. It was all there. I mean, I wouldn't go so far as to suggest that the affinity for doppelgängers or negritude were a part of this sibling of Shandyism, but one can't have everything in life and we're not going to get bureaucratic about this. We'll discuss the radical relation to suicide that was central to late Shandyism in a bit.

*

Goliardos: paperback, single-colour cover (purple, navy blue, pink), black and white print on standard bond paper. Ornate, barely legible fonts. Layers upon layers, visually baroque. A fanzine through and through, but we prefer to call them chapbooks, thank you very much. Portable art.

Flipping through the pages of a Goliardo means finding text surrounded by arrangements of classical images of nymphs with vampire wings, abductions of Pysche with planets in the background, an outrageous number of female nudes—mostly nineteenth-century paintings but also, on a few horrifying occasions, montages made from photographs with a vaguely porno vibe offset by layers of cyberpunk. Extreme sexuality.

Change the design? Impossible. I tried to convince him, as did his students and God only knows who else over all those years. My father was steadfast, or obstinate, in his position that this was the one and only correct design for Goliardos. In every sense, a cultivation of the art of insolence.

My ex and I spoke often about the beauty of simple books,

like those German editions with their minimal, elegant covers. About how Goliardos should move in that direction, tone down its screeching baroque. Luckily, if there's one thing my father fought against his entire life it was against normalising himself to, in his words, fit in with the mainstream. With the bourgeoisie. In that respect, at least, he was consistent. In an act of pure love for pulp, he made ugliness his chosen aesthetic. I don't know if I'm reading too much into things, but today I'm glad he insisted on leaving it that way and can finally appreciate the sui generis madness of those fanzines I was so embarrassed of back then. I can also see in them a disinterest in the pre-packaged and hierarchical sense of grand statements, which are all tied to a legitimacy afforded by the status quo. But there's another way to read that Shandy principle. Alfonso, who was his student and friend for many years—and who at some point distanced himself from him because, in his words, "I loved him so much that I didn't want to end up hating him"—adds: "It was also because self-publishing was our comfort zone." They didn't need to face those menacing corporate publishers and the "no" they kept always at the ready.

*

My parents were still married when Goliardos got its start, but much of the group's history belongs to the period when they were no longer a couple. Alfonso tells me: "I think what set your mother's teeth on edge was the time and resources your father put into Goliardos and the chaos he left everywhere, boxes and boxes of books. We used to say to him, 'Hey, Pascal—don't you have kids or something?'" Later, when my parents divorced, Alfonso was among those who came by to take my father's things from the apartment, his face grey with shame; he was also present for the magical moment when my father took the bookshelves. I don't know how much Goliardos had to do with the divorce and I'm not going to look into it now, but it does seem notable to me that my father never had another long-term relationship. A bachelor machine. I'd love to believe this was because of his commitment to that precept of Shandyism, but I don't think so. I think everything became hard for him after the separation. Alfonso speculates that he never got over (forgive me for what I'm about to write) his *elf*, who was in part my mother, and in much greater part a fantasy.

His inability to mourn the loss seems symptomatic of his traditional masculinity. In the end, my father had something else in common with the Shandys, and it's far less festive than the list above: his machismo, which manifested itself everywhere—both inside him and in his interactions with the outside world.

*

Here, too, in *A Brief History of Portable Literature*, I see a reflection of the patriarchy we continue to inhabit. The Shandys consisted of a whole bunch of famous men with a femme fatale (sic sic sic) tossed in here and there for good measure. From the distinction alone, you can tell who is who. My favourite among the artists included in this category is Georgia O'Keeffe, the North American whose flowers, painted with sweeping, gradient brushstrokes, are pure sensuality. In the novel, I don't know if also in real life, it was she who introduced the Shandy secret society to the concept of extreme sexuality. "'Libido,' Picabia tells us the femme fatale declared while filing her nails, 'ought to be separated from its genetic purpose, which we understand as reproduction; one's own satisfaction is the only thing that should be sought. In a word, to copulate for pure pleasure, never thinking about progeny or other trifles. This is what I understand by extreme sexuality.'" With this, asserts the narrator, she uncouples this set of artists from maternity, says the narrator. Very convenient, especially considering that several of the men in the group did indeed have progeny.

Portable artists, as the members of the society called themselves, were bachelor machines because they knew that love was a prison, while they were ever-so-free. I read it again and repeat to myself: how convenient.

O'Keeffe is deadly because she exists, and in her existence sparks attractions she does not reciprocate, particularly in the pathetic poet Jacques Rigaut, an ardent proponent of suicide who, no matter how pointless (and irksome) the gesture, decides to follow her to New York and stalk her. He even takes out ads in the newspaper.

The idea of the femme fatale, the woman who could destroy you, is one of the more subtly misogynist tropes in literature. One of my father's favourites. Lamia, the Ancient Greek demon hidden in the body of a beautiful woman who approached men deep in the woods. Or the sirens, who would lure them towards madness with their dulcet song. All the products of this culture that fears female sexuality and yet feels irresistibly drawn to it. The women who mark the Shandy secret society are femmes fatales because every woman becomes one, to a certain extent, the moment she decides to prioritise herself, her art and her occupation over a man.

*

Femmes fatales everywhere, like a mirage. When my father was alive, I had two big fears. The first, which I'll talk about later, ended with his death. The second, which continues to twist my insides, still flutters over his corpse of dust. Women. My father and us women.

A friend tells me how her seventy-year-old father writes to twenty-year-old women on Facebook. She knows that more than one has blocked him, and she often feels ashamed. She can't do anything about it, and the knowledge that he's doing it is painful enough without the added shame of being judged by other women for not intervening. She even feels bad about him being blocked, even though she knows he deserves it. Did my father do something similar and I just didn't know?

Eight years before he died, my father decided that the creative writing workshop he gave every Thursday—which was, basically, the centre of his life—would be for women only. He was a fifty-year-old man teaching a class to women writers, nearly all of whom were young. The first time I saw the ad announcing the workshop's "separatist" approach, I froze. What the hell was this? I decided to ignore it, to act like it was just a bad joke.

When the second announcement went out six months later, I couldn't turn a blind eye. He asked me, along with all his other contacts, to help circulate it. I needed to ask why he'd changed the dynamic of the class. "Because I've been giving this workshop for twenty years and I can count on one hand the women who have taken it," he replied. I accepted his answer and soothed my heartburn with a cup of herbal tea. On one hand, I was terrified no one would sign up. The image of my father sitting alone in the Centro Cultural José Martí with a bag full of books to give out—waiting thirty minutes, then an hour, for anyone to show—turned my stomach. On the other hand, I was afraid that women *would* attend a workshop led by this older gentleman who loved erotic literature more than anything in the world, and that they would feel uncomfortable.

I try to judge him less and understand him more, but it's so hard. At the same time, who am I to say what makes someone else uncomfortable? Isn't that condescending? Particularly when the women who studied with him still speak warmly of him to this day. A Pascalised shandy for each of them.

*

While I read about the suicidal figures who pursued O'Keeffe even unto their death, I remember my earliest encounters (and missed encounters) with feminism. My maternal grandmother Margarita studied Literature and Philosophy (it was all one department) at the Universidad Nacional Autónoma de México in the 1950s. At the home that used to be hers, there's a small collection of Simone de Beauvoir's writings to which I never paid much attention.

The first time I tried to read *The Second Sex*, I was twenty years old and had taken it with me to the beach. That was the vacation when I discovered the concept of "beach reads" by exploring their opposite: "books you'll carry around pointlessly and ruin with salt air." I didn't make it ten pages in. Meanwhile, I'd read *Memoirs of a Dutiful Daughter* when I was a teenager and more than anything it had been a sweet balm that helped me fall asleep after a few pages. What spectacular naps I enjoyed thanks to Simone; how I marvelled at the sea while ignoring her book. Not so many years ago, I learned that several of my grandmother's editions of Beauvoir were gifts from my father. Giving books: his patented method of getting in someone's good graces. I find it charming that this gesture brought them closer, even if only a little. They were not avowed feminists. My grandmother was a (wonderful) woman of her time—shy, sweet, with a bit of a temper—who gave up her studies when she married. My father was a (sensitive) macho. Maybe they unintentionally encouraged one another be different. Maybe they even succeeded, a little.

*

My copy of *Memoirs of a Dutiful Daughter* also came from him, but I guess he never imagined I would take my feminism so far. He probably didn't think feminism would go so far in the world in general. Despite being a child of the seventies, a leftist with the heart of an activist, this new wave... flustered him, to say the least. There were many, many poems about the violence of this terrible country and the sonorous bellow of Mexico City, but not one word about the mistreatment of all the women who suddenly burst forth like a geyser of collective conscience.

*

As I read Vila-Matas, I interrogate each of my steps. Am I writing a patriarchal book? Does writing within this system mean the answer is always yes? Is my book about books, in which I talk about men and one man in particular, just a monument to the phallus? Does it matter? I don't know how to answer these questions. It's obvious that not every act by a woman escapes the logic of machismo, just like it's obvious that women do misogynistic things all the time. But I don't think we should feel obligated to be feminists all the time, as if it were an identity that dignifies us, rather than—as I've preferred to see it for a while, now—a project of social transformation and a tool, among many, for analysing the world.

*

A guy told me once, as a compliment, that I don't write like a woman.

An ex-boyfriend who never read women told me once that there weren't any books out there that "described the experience of being a woman," and that I should write one.

A male friend told me once that I should submit my writing to a prize just for women because there were so few women writers and they were all so bad that I was sure to win.

A woman told me once, as an insult, that I don't write like a woman.

To a certain extent, I have been each of them at one point or another.

I need to ask myself why I write what I write, and why I read what I read. I wonder if the male writers from that generation do the same. If they find themselves subject to the same kind of scrutiny when they decide what to write about or read. I wonder if we ask these questions of them as much as we ask them of ourselves.[11] What a way to squeeze us dry, like a lime.

11 OURSELVES: The collective feminine "nosotras" is, as we know, a rhetorical device—there are so many different realities that the political subject "woman" is just a projection joining together that which is impossible to unite.

66

*

And anyway, none of this is a guarantee because we're all standing on foundations laid by centuries of patriarchy. My father, for example, was deeply and honestly in favour of gender equality. When #MeToo blew up, he wrote to our family group chat:

Sure. We've been doing it for decades. When I insisted some twenty years ago that women should get involved, a few cynics thought it was because I wanted some action. What a joke. En Goliardos, only *** and *** ever needed to be reined in—not because we were worried about a scandal but because it's bullshit to go around bothering people like that. It's not a policy, it's just common sense.

*

Sometimes I fantasise about discussing this with other women writers, asking them to share some part of their relationships with their fathers. I want to know what they think, whether they feel those gender dynamics in their gut and in their chest. I want to look them in the eye and ask them, with my heart in my throat:

What do you feel (if and) when you catch your father gawking at a young woman?

Did your father also make comments about your body that left scars?

Are you scared your father will be cancelled online one day, too?

How do you strike the balance between understanding and not excusing?

Have you ever wept in fear because your father doesn't take care of himself? Because he's such a man's man that he doesn't need to see a doctor?

Have you ever wished you didn't have a father?

Did your father remember your birthday when you were little? Do you find it hard to love him?

The shame is overwhelming.

*

But I also think something's missing from the story. That whole bachelor machine business is never enough. Bachelor machines want all the love with none of the pain; they long for someone to wrap themselves around at night who won't make them promise to tame the monster in their chest.[12] Things other than pleasure are always concealed within extreme sexuality—or rather, the pleasure isn't only physical, it feeds on so much: status, power, intimacy, vulnerability. And concealed within the disinterest in grand statements is so often a profound fear of failure.

I do have a talent for sucking the life out of poetry.

*

I've killed my desire to read with all this thinking, so I search the internet for my father's poems and find a video tribute that Jessica Robles, his former student, made after he died. I

---

12   CHEST MONSTER: Mine has tentacles that reach my pelvis and strong arms that squeeze my thorax, especially on those cloudy days when melancholy stirs it from its peaceful slumber. It vomits things from my mouth, shoots fire from my eyes. Sometimes it enjoys itself.

begin to shake and feel The Pain approaching. I'm writing at someone else's house, and they keep interrupting me; I have to pretend I'm fine but I'm about to scream or start crying, whichever comes first. His student talks about how generous he was and says that only he could have gone the way he did: reading. "Pascal taught me to appreciate poetry," she says and talks about the exhibits they'd seen together. We'd grown so distant by his final years that his students saw him much more than I did. I knew several of them, a few went to his funeral together. Even seeing them and listening to them, even reading all the beautiful things they wrote about him when he died, I still judge him for teaching a workshop for women only. I still think badly of him, like when he posted photos of those visits to museums with his students (he always posted pictures of everything). Now I hear her saying that poetry made her cry for the first time because of him. I'm a little jealous of her and her total lack of prejudice.

*

We're the daughters of progressive machos if we're lucky, and of macho machos if we're not. The generational shift has opened vast fissures between fathers and daughters. My father wasn't particularly macho, but he did have his moments. Like telling me, with all the authority vested in him by his huge belly, that I needed to lose some weight—even pointing out when my teenage pants had gotten too tight. Or like calling women crazy when they didn't act the way he thought they should. May those who are without sin cast the first stones.

*

Back home I get my fingers on paper, which is like saying I get my feet under me. I've discovered a genre of books about the personal libraries of writers (including a few women). Entire volumes dedicated to this, and it seems like a way to understand the writing better, a map through a creative labyrinth. The news is accompanied by an uncomfortable confession. For years, I've been going back and forth about whether I consider my father a writer. All evidence indicates that he was. His novels and poetry collections are right there, in case other testimonies aren't enough. Even so, it's hard for me.

*

A few of the women writers in my father's library:
- Margo Glantz
- Emily Dickinson
- Cristina Peri-Rossi
- Susan Sontag
- Ana Clavel
- Sappho
- Cristina Rivera Garza
- Rosa Montero
- Rosa Beltrán
- Clyo Mendoza
- Anne Carson

As a ballpark figure, I'd say books by women constitute about twenty percent of his library. I don't know if that's a lot or a little.

*

Then I think about how many books by women were even published before, how many women were driven mad because they wanted to dedicate themselves to anything outside the bounds of traditional gender norms. I search my memory—because there's nothing in my notebooks—for any register of women I read while I was in school. A few assigned readings I do remember: *The Alchemist* by Paolo Coelho, *The Truce* by Mario Benedetti, *The Little Prince* by Antoine de Saint-Exupéry, *The Turn of the Screw* by Henry James. A heterogenous selection that moves between countries, qualities and genres, but which is consistent on one point: not a single woman. Digging a bit deeper, I realise that all of my literature teachers were women—and we still never read a single text written by a woman: not Rosario Castellanos, not Josefina Vicens, not Elena Garro. Maybe a little snippet of Sor Juana, that bare minimum required by all educational programmes, but nothing more. Compared to that, my father was a trailblazer. Which isn't saying much.

Violence isn't only action—it's also inaction. When the Romans wanted to punish a bad emperor, general or public figure, they would apply the *damnatio memoriae*, an unusual process that involved erasing all trace of the person, removing their face from statues and coins. The worst punishment is being forgotten. In the case of literature, there's no need to rely on deliberate acts of annihilation. There are many subtle mechanisms that determine whether a work is allowed into the canon—or not. The destiny of a text, once published, usually depends on forces beyond the person who wrote it. Most immediately, it depends on its ability to circulate among readers and reviewers (here, all sorts of power dynamics come into play). Later, it will depend on the text remaining in our collective memory through official and unofficial channels.

The canon is a social construct that we naturalise far more often than we should. It's not some self-regulating mystical entity with built-in quality control. It's an accumulation of prejudices and preferences that different forces consolidate into a selection of desirable aesthetic elements. The canon is a manifestation of the idiosyncrasies of an era, which is why it changes from one period to the next. Until recently, it was predominantly male and bourgeois. Some things have changed, others have not. Books like *A Brief History of Portable Literature* are delicious sweets confected from the canon itself. They make mythologies of its constituent parts.

*

We shouldn't forget that *A Brief History of Portable Literature* (the pleasure of typing that title out each time) wasn't always a celebrated work of literature. When it was published in 1985, Vila-Matas wasn't the award-winning writer he is today. The book was declared ridiculous by, precisely, the literary mainstream. This inspired gem of humour, imagination and irony was completely misunderstood in a context that celebrated sweeping realist narratives. But that didn't stop Vila-Matas, and to this day his writing retains that spark, that ability to reinvent tradition. A Pascalised shandy for Enrique Vila-Matas.

*

With this delicious sweet on my tongue, I ask myself questions I can't answer. Can you really take someone who was raised up to his neck in the canon, in married bachelor machines, in extreme sexuality only for men, in women labelled as femmes fatales, and ask him to change his entire emotional configuration from one day to the next? Questions that set my skin ablaze, that spark contradictory answers. If I could go back in time and be someone else, a less clumsy version of myself, I would start by asking my father how he feels about all this instead of pointing my finger at him.

*

I think that asking this question a thousand times over the years could have prevented disasters. How hard to be a man and feel like you can't answer it honestly, like you can't be anything but a stoic monolith. One day, no one knows exactly when, my father simply gave up. He started leaving the house less and less, stopped seeing his friends and became just a disembodied voice on social media. He barely went to work.

One day his boss, a person I didn't know, called me. He said that my father hadn't turned in any work lately, that he wasn't even showing up to the office. His boss held a government post and was fond of my father because they'd known each other for years. He told me he wanted to see me. When I hung up, I felt an urge to vomit. I still do, to this day.

You can't control someone else's depression. I want to copy that phrase over and over until I commit it to memory.

Maybe that's why I began to notice, at the end of his life, an upward inflection in the way he talked, like a child trying to make a friend, like a question asked with just a trace of reticence. He was trying. I was, too, but my resentment was too strong. An archaeology of the misfortune of not reconciling in time, despite one's best intentions.

And an archaeology aimed at trying to understand whether

he knew his life was ending, or if he was even thinking, in the style of a few of those early Shandys, that it might be time to abandon this storm-tossed ship?

With this other taste in my mouth, I close *A Brief History of Portable Literature*.

*

What am I doing in these pages? Am I, too, mythologising Pascal? Defaming Juan Manuel? In a video less than four minutes long, Dipak Pallana describes the rituals, life and philosophy of his father, Kumar Pallana. Kumar became famous after appearing in several of Wes Anderson's movies; despite not having much screen time, his roles were indispensable to the magic of those films. *The Rituals of Kumar Pallana* was shot when the actor, yogi, acrobat, entertainer, etc. was ninety-three years old. He looks healthy, strong, agile. On screen, he prepares cups of chai that make my mouth water.

Facing his son's camera, Kumar invites us to live a simple life, because with greater simplicity comes fewer worries. Kumar meditates, teaches yoga classes, spins plates, smiles, makes jokes, laughs hard and recommends a good trip to the bathroom every morning. I don't know anyone who hasn't loved the old man at least a little after watching this video. This small monument to his father is an example of the stylistic beauty that tenderness can achieve.

Dipak portrays Kumar in warm tones, showing his biggest smiles, fondest moments and greatest achievements. If Kumar was rude to a hotel receptionist, if at some point he hit his son until he cried, if making his chai too watery ever drove him to throw random objects at the door in a fury, this video gives no hint of it. A small statue of our time in video form: four minutes of pure love.

Kumar Pallana died the following year, at the age of ninety-four. It's hard to believe that someone so full of life already had one foot in the grave. Maybe among the material that ended up on the cutting room floor was a coughing fit, a loss of bladder control or the request for a moment's rest when nonagenarian weariness would eat into his bones. All weakness and error omitted.

As I write this book, I see myself standing before a balance. Its scales teeter between my desire to speak from the gut, to describe my father with all his sharp edges and his failings—because he was those things, too (he was especially those things, my still-angry gut tells me)—and to render in words *The Rituals of Juan Manuel García Junco* with all of Dipak's sweetness. Sometimes, melancholy invites me to write my own monument, one that softens father's sharp edges, and in so doing keeps others from judging him as harshly as I have. To make a hero. A misunderstood poet versus the world. A love letter.

*

Meanwhile, all I have left is this knot in my stomach that I really should begin to untie. As if that were possible. I put the book back on the shelf and think it would be better to go further back to where it all began, before Shandyism and all the rest of it.

75

From: Aura García-Junco <aura.garciajunco@gmail.com>
Date: Fri, Sept 6, 2013, 18:33
To: Pascal
Rumour has it you're not answering your phone.
Your dear mother is worried sick; report in!

From: H. Pascal <hpascalien@yahoo.com.mx>
Date: Thurs, Oct 10, 2013, 16:24
To: me
Rumour has it you have a new phone number and haven't shared it with your dear father. Why might that be?

From: Aura García-Junco <aura.garciajunco@gmail.com>
Date: Thurs, Oct 10, 2013, 17:36
To: Pascal
Haha because I always thought I'd get it back,
but I officially lost hope at some point.

THIRD: MRS. WERNER SUDDENLY FELL ILL ONE NIGHT

Part of this library has always been there. Its spines, of incongruent dimensions and bearing typographies in danger of extinction, stand out among the other books, with their identical fonts printed on plasticised card stock. It currently occupies an entire corner of the bookshelf; from here, in my habitual passive contemplation, I can see their browned pages and can almost smell the century-old dust they hold.

Assorted books, various authors, various publishers, various dates of publication. Net contents: 15 bedraggled textbooks (subjects also various).

Frau Werner war in einer Nacht plötzlich krank geworden. Deutsches Lesebuch für Grundschulen, II Ausgabe.

If my inability to read gothic typeface isn't playing tricks on me, the book in my hands is called *Blütenflocken. Gedichte von Luise Rophamel.* I wish I could convey in words the beauty of this volume, but nothing compares to feeling its heft. I was first drawn to it by its gilded lettering and the illustration on its grey cover: pink cherry blossoms, black birds and a tiny ship enclosed in a circle of delicate lattice. Words don't itch nearly as much as the decades of dust covering my hands and spreading through my lungs, either. On its exquisite title page, I read that it was printed in 1895 and that it cost eighty cents (in what currency?). After that, two hundred pages of poetry in that font used for every nineteenth-century German book.

I don't know German. Neither did my father. I've tried to learn it so many times that another attempt would be an insult to the language, to my ability to be honest with myself and to language acquisition in general. I agree wholeheartedly with Mark Twain's assertion that life is too short to learn German, but also a little with Borges, who called it the most beautiful language.[13]

This mute volume is a representative of the Embassy of

---

13   WHO CALLED IT: The most profane form of lying is quoting Borges by ear—just because one should, just because doing so is in such good taste that it's actually in the worst possible taste.

Goodwill, a title I assigned a subgroup of the shelves I'm currently reviewing.

Family: Bibliotheca Patris.

Genus: Bibliotheca Antiqua.

Species: Liber germanus inutilis (Embassy of Goodwill)

A well-meaning section of the bookshelves that contains everything from grammar textbooks to indecipherable poems, which my father kept all these years for some reason, though I never saw him study German. I guess the dream of learning it in your sleep never dies, or else at some point the habit of seeing certain evidently useless books becomes stronger than the awareness that you'll need to haul them in some future move as merely ornamental objects. The book's beauty makes me happy, but I find its hermetism depressing, a sign of my lack of discipline.

Blütenflocken. Gedichte von Luise Rophamel. A Google search for Luise Rophamel yields no results. Some unknown nineteenth-century poet whose work didn't make the leap into the great digital encyclopaedia. Does that make her book more or less valuable? I can't decide. If I could read it, I could judge for myself what's worth keeping.

*

My father—who will be my only (imprecise) source of information in order to avoid multiple versions—always said that his grandmother was a German who smoked cigars and occasionally fell asleep with one in her mouth. The family legend, as he tells it is that his Oma died in her nineties, still as strong as an ox. This is, without a doubt, scientific proof that smoking is harmless. And from there, I suppose, was born a long line of inveterate smokers who only relinquish the practice when, let's say, they suffer a near-fatal heart attack or die.

My father tried to give up smoking the same year he met his end. Not even when my baby brother was diagnosed with asthma and we needed to set up humidifiers around the house had this been a possibility. My mother quit cold turkey one day, with nothing but her determination, but my father would still get as angry as ever when I asked him not to smoke in the car. When my brother and I cleared out his apartment, we took down the pictures hanging on his walls (a reproduction of a Brueghel the Elder, kitsch fairies, a photo of José Revueltas, another taken by Juan Rulfo, an engraving by Eko, etc.), revealing their negative images. The rest of the wall's surface was such an intense tarry yellow that you forgot there had once been another colour underneath. Only when we removed the pictures did we realise how years of cigarette smoke can change the tone of surfaces and people.

His dedication to smoking is why I hate cigarettes as much as I do, why I've never taken a single drag of one. That inescapable, invasive vice.

*

Illness is the clearest reminder that we are bodies, and I wonder what it's like to live with the permanent memento mori that is an incurable disease. I found out that my father needed heart surgery because he told my aunt at my book presentation, and my aunt told my mother, and my mother told me after he died. Whenever I asked him how he was, he said he was fine. At least we were consistent in our incapacity to communicate the pains of our bodies and souls.

I wonder how one thinks about one's body when it lacks

oxygen due to years of smoking and a heart that can't pump enough blood anymore. I wonder if the constantly swollen feet, the inguinal hernias, the aching knee and the impossibility of clear thought, if all the painful trips to the bathroom, if the difficulty urinating, if the insomnia, if...

I ask myself straight out: if this is life, might death be better?

My father would suddenly fall into a state that was half dozing, half dim-witted. He lost his spark and his interest in arguing—or partially, at least. His illness was a curtain that separated him from the world and rendered him untranslatable.

*

The antique books section (aka the Bibliotheca Antiqua)[14] is full of dishevelled spines and yellowed pages. A fungus might force the early retirement of a few volumes; naturally, I have to wear gloves when I look at them, lest the unwelcome guests settle into my skin or one of my eyes. A third eye from new-found wisdom, or partial blindness with lasting consequences?

Each of the books in German (Liber germanus inutilis or the Embassy of Goodwill) has a numbered piece of paper stuck between its first pages, seemingly to keep the volumes in order: 117, 100, 85. Nearly all bear a stamp that offers a clue to this mystery: Eigentum von M. García-Junco. M for Marcelino. These books belonged to my great-grandfather, Marcelino García-Junco Payán. The man's personal library immediately

---

14   ANTIQUA: What is so redundant and cliché about naming old things in Latin? Dear, dear Latin, you have a bad reputation and stink of dust, but how lovely to seize any excuse, even the most forced, to stroke your tarnished silver hair.

reveals something about him: his organisation. But is it his or my grandfather, Juan Manuel's? Because, asserts my inner amateur sleuth, the person who stamped the books is not necessarily the same person who numbered them.

Most members of the Embassy are written in a gothic font completely unintelligible to mere mortals from this century. The typography used for German books until the second half of the twentieth century is called Fraktur because each letter requires more than one stroke: its principal feature is that the O has several lines on the left side and one lone round line on the right. The font is dark, dense and jumbled.

Maybe these books could teach me through the memorisation of didactic phrases: Frau Werner war in einer Nacht plötzlich krank geworden. Mrs. Werner suddenly fell ill one night.

The transition from Fraktur to Antiqua—another gothic typeface, though a bit more easy-going—had to be decreed by Hitler in 1934. Even so, the fracture was so deeply rooted that no one wanted to give it up. Antiqua wouldn't be used widely until 1941, when an official mandate explicitly prohibited its gothic sister. Nearly every book in this section is printed in Fraktur, and only a few in Antiqua. All are equally illegible.

If I were to try to learn to play chess with the book *Schachstrategie. Einführung in den Geist der Praktischen Partie von Eduard Lasker* (number 116), I would have to overcome three obstacles: my lack of talent with strategic games, the language and the font, though the book is perfect for the instruction of certain indispensable terms like König, Reihe and zurück (king, row and backwards or back). Suddenly it doesn't seem so farfetched that you might be able to learn German and chess at the same time or that, on the basis of what you know about chess, German might naturally sink in through your pores. When I was an undergraduate, someone told us that Werner Jaeger, the great German philologist and author of *Paideia: The Ideals of Greek Culture*, acquired his perfect Spanish by reading *Don Quixote*. I'll never know whether this is an elaboration on the documented fact that Freud learned Spanish to achieve the same end (though not *in the process* of reading *Don Quixote*). This capacity to learn a language independently for the love of a cultural monument is a cliché of the Man of Genius.

I wonder if this collection was somehow planned, or if the happenstance of passing years simply left him with this curious assortment of German texts. A list of hopes and desires? "Maybe this year I'll become an expert at chess, and next year I'll learn Ancient Greek."

A surprise that puts me in as good a mood as receiving plushy pyjamas from my grandmother for Christmas: I pull two beat-up volumes from among all the dust, an Ancient Greek reader and one for Latin. I love this approach to learning classical languages—starting with simple, intuitive texts that get progressively more complex without much explanation. I'm also thrilled by the *Deutsches Lesebuch für Volksschulen*, a book for German children that works the same way: increasingly difficult texts, poems and illustrations, organised thematically. It's meant for lower school students, but it proves too much for me.

My hands twitch with joy and hives. I should keep my time with these books to a bare minimum—they're beautiful potential killers, all.

*

I pick up volume 117 of this Lost Library: Ostermann-Müllers. *Lateinisches Übungsbuch*. 1919, Teubner. Eigentum von M. García-Junco.

What must have gone through my father's mind when I entered the nerdiest of all the already-nerdy degree programmes in literature? I imagine I must have informed him with an unspoken confidence that I would graduate. I don't remember him verbalising any enthusiasm, but I'm sure he asked me all sorts of questions with a gleam in his eye. Classics. I spent five years reading fragmented texts in other languages, often more drawn to what I didn't understand in them than to what I did. Our fetish for ancient things, for the impenetrable wall that the passing centuries erect around these works, whether we like it or not.

I'm surprised by how easy it is to project our thinking onto the texts we read, making them our own. Classical texts are subject to a dual phenomenon: we read them from our own subjectivity in the present, so this translation is inevitable. And yet, their authors are somewhat impervious to our deep-seated prejudices because they're so distant from us that it can be hard to connect with them.[15] It takes a whole series of prologues to begin to feel closer to them, though no salve can mend the distance entirely. Blessed are the writers of historical fiction, for theirs is the kingdom of imaginative empathy. Blessed was my father, a member of that exclusive club, who—when he

---

15   THEM: This "them" is almost exclusively male because the only apple left on that tree is Sappho—all the other women were lost over the years, never to be recovered. Athena, you were that mother who let her sons do as they pleased and kept her daughters hidden.

was still young and inclined to spend years on a single book—wrote a few historical novels with his own particular bent: erotic tales set in Imperial China, medieval quests for the Holy Grail.

*

There is a leather-bound edition of Hermann und Dorothea from around 1920. Part Tischbein's 1786 portrait of Goethe appears slightly off-centre on the first page. Lavish borders around the title. This diminutive volume, Google informs me, is worth a mind-boggling nine euros. Therefore, according to its price, it should not be categorised as an antique but rather as junk. When I brought the library home, two friends helped me find a place for everything. One of those friends was a guy, and after all the old books had been stashed in one corner, he said bluntly, "They might be treasures or they might be trash. Sell them fast because they've probably got mould that can spread to your other books." Naturally, I sold nothing fast; I couldn't care less about mould and even hated the world for the suggestion that any book with so many years behind it could be considered junk. I will, without a doubt, regret my lack of resolve when one of those spores finds its ways through the cracks. For the moment, though, I love poring over those Latin and Greek readers, pretending to be a young German girl learning the language with rhymes and leafing through illustrated junk with hieroglyphic contents. These are the books that become permanent fixtures in a nostalgic library, the ones you can't get rid of, no matter how useless they are, unless you're willing to tear out a piece of your heart.

Though it bears no stamp of ownership, *Hermann und Dorothea* contains a little paper label marked with the number

85, which officially declares it a member of the original collection belonging to my grandfather or my great-grandfather.

Old books awaken a cheesy spirit of investigation, like in *The Red Violin*, or worse, *The Da Vinci Code*. One can imagine how much their blind eyes have seen; how much they know and have experienced. Objects four times our age that have lived in so many homes they've lost count. There's a mystery to them. In my father's life alone, these books passed through at least seven residences. Before that, they crossed the sea in a roving journey. They are relics of a family history that grows more distant by the day—their value is sentimental rather than monetary.

The fetish for dust. I wonder what sense there is in loving a bunch of old books. What sense there is in preserving old things in general.

*

Juan Manuel García Junco Rohde was a translator. He died of a heart attack when my father was twelve years old. More precisely, he died of the unfortunate combination of circumstances that is suffering a heart attack while driving and then crashing into a brick wall that opens your skull.

My grandmother still cries over him as if it were yesterday when she arrived at the hospital and was told that her husband was undergoing brain surgery and probably wouldn't pull through. The man spent seven nights in intensive care, on the fence between sticking with this bittersweet existence and throwing in the towel. From one day to the next, his family—which consisted of my grandmother Tiche, my two uncles, my father and my aunt—went from middle class to impoverished. Next came the whole shameful spectacle of pulling the children out of private school and sending them to public middle school, making ends meet on my grandmother's teaching salary and whatever charity their other relatives were inclined to offer. Getting used to living without a father to provide for them.

My father liked to tell the story of how his uncle Marcelino—who unfortunately did not die young—was such a tyrant that when my grandfather died he allowed the family to continue living in the house that had been left to them, but only if they kept to the first floor. The slight disadvantage to this arrangement was that there was no bathroom. For all intents and purposes, he took their home. To top it off, he was racist through and through and used to hang Nazi flags from the roof. The family hated the idea that Marcelino's outrageous behaviour would call attention to Berthel, my German great-grandmother, who had nothing to do with all that. Though she came from a family of construction workers who were most likely collaborators, she herself appeared to have no interest in national socialism and had been living in Mexico for decades, cut off from it all. Marcelino's bad reputation lives on in the family as a kind of metaphor for the evils any lineage can have. I suppose there's a figure like him in every family history.

As befit her German origins, my father called his grandmother Oma. His grandfather, by extension, was Opa, even though he was Mexican. More glamorous that way, I guess. My great-grandfather Marcelino received his doctorate in chemistry from the University of Berlin. It would have been a typical study abroad story were it not for the fact that his was set in the period between the First and Second World Wars. He lived in a castle (German currency was that weak at the time) and came back to Mexico with his fiancée Berthel, who would never return to Europe. For the purposes of this story (our family history), she was addressed as "Oma" and was, apparently, a fiery woman. She made cakes of dried fruit that came in a wooden box where the pastry would sit for months before softening enough that it wouldn't endanger the teeth of anyone who took a bite. Going by the caricature, I imagine her smoking a cigar even as she kneaded, working the dough of a recipe handed down over generations, precise measurements in the hands of an expert. An internet revelation: no one told me that my great-grandmother had been a chemist, too. I would have loved to ask my father more about her; I'm sure he would've had great stories to share.[16] Instead, all I have are snapshots recounted by my grandmother Tiche of the woman grumbling in a Spanish heavy with *rr*s any time someone asked for one of her recipes. Aside from a couple of formulas for Streuselkuchen and cookies, the miser took them all to the grave with her.

*

My living room is inhabited by an iron Singer sewing machine set into a wooden table pockmarked by years of watering the plants that currently rest on it. It belonged to my grandmother's grandmother. My grandmother mentions it often because for a while she wanted it back after my parents' divorce. Impossible. I'd always had my eye on it. In my childhood home, it was the telephone table. As a little girl, I spent countless hours playing with its pedal, which was still connected to the machine by a leather band, and grew obsessed with

---

16   TO HAVE GREAT STORIES: To invent memories that have no basis in concrete reality but are instead grounded in affect.

the mystery inside its wooden casing. When I moved into my own place, its many kilos of Art Nouveau iron came with me. The internet tells me that it now qualifies as an antique, but it doesn't tell me what to do with it, so the beautiful Singer sits patiently in my hallway, holding an enormous plant and a few odds and ends in its drawers: catnip, assorted screwdrivers, a cup-and-ball, fifty pesos.

For a while, it held another antique officially recognised as such: a Remington 12 typewriter that was given to me by a friend on my twenty-eighth birthday and which fits right in with the other inhabitants here in the sense that it sometimes stirs wonder, but often just gets in the way. A decorative treat for the eyes, it reminds me of my cats because of its silent presence and the quantity of hair it accumulates between its keys. The difference is that it has existed far longer than any of the living beings in this household. I estimate, without any evidence or specialised knowledge beyond the results of an internet search, that it's probably from around 1920. The history of my particular monstrosity is even harder to pin down than that of the books in the Embassy, about which I have at least some information.

I imagine the Remington in glamorous melodramas, sharing its life with some mid-century writer; I picture her pressing its sonorous keys to create a series of complex, ungainly books that are still in the bottom of a drawer in the house of her grandson, a dentist with no idea what to do with the legacy of his eccentric grandmother. The most likely scenario, however, is that the typewriter lived in an accounting office, or that a small-time politician in the PRI used it for drafting repugnant documents, but I refuse to fall into those bleak corners of my imagination.

Writing on a typewriter when you're not accustomed to it

is like running a marathon after training with only one-mile runs. I search for ways to use it: letters, first drafts of short texts, statements of gratitude. I can't find any. I don't know how to change the ribbon, either. In fact, I don't know how to do anything with it but look at it and imagine the names of its former owners. The sewing machine's leather band has been broken since I moved it in, so even though it would probably still work, there's no way to get it running. Both artefacts are so heavy they can barely be moved, even within the same room. They simply age, demand care, fall apart bit by bit.

I guess that some people would see them as the first things to get rid of; that they would appear entirely devoid of value, and their history would be more an annoyance than an asset. The line between treasure and trash is just a question of fetish.

Antiques, inheritances, stories and uselessness often go hand in hand. I should start a "Gleeful Geezer" corner and unite the books and machines in an anachronistic orgy. They probably wouldn't recognisze one another as equals since they belong to different periods—the ones from 1900 would cold-shoulder the ones from the roaring '30s, the ones from 1950 would turn their nose up at the sight of 1890s Gedichte—though to our eyes the past is often one, and the category "antique" swallows up objects divided by a century or more. Nonetheless, *Hermann und Dorothea* could live happily here in this corner, at ease, not needing to worry that someone might notice their measly nine-euro price tag.

*

My father likes to tell the story, though I wouldn't swear to its veracity, of how some very serious men once knocked on the door looking for Opa. They wanted to inform him that the

Nobel committee was considering him for the prize on the basis of his discoveries in the field of synthesising hormones. Oma opened the door, asked what they wanted, and—without blinking an eye—told them all to go to hell.

Ah, legends of former family glory, accounts of a heroic past that both elevate and pressure later generations. They're nothing but a pain in the ass.

Unsurprisingly, Opa was a neurotic fellow who prohibited all noise in the house while he was working and would explode with rage if any child dared to insert their youth into his territory. As we all know, the Man of Genius must be intolerant and ready to take the belt to anyone who sullies his pristine intellectual spaces.

It is also said that Opa rose at five in the morning every day of his adult life to pursue his studies. I don't know if this superpower is connected to his screaming at every innocent intrusion, but I admire his dedication.

*

My father died of a heart attack,[17] his father died of a heart attack, my uncle had a heart attack and barely survived it. If I were my brother, I would swaddle my heart like it was made of glass.

Frau Werner war in einer Nacht plötzlich krank geworden.

---

17   TO DIE OF A HEART ATTACK: A heart attack that might be a winter's gust through the soul.

*

In *Papyrus*, Irene Vallejo tells us that to choose is, in some ways, to protect. To choose is to protect. I choose these books and give them a home, and they give me a home in return. I did not destroy his library, I saved some of his books. Come to think of it, this is how I imagine the process by which my father ended up with those books that his father left to him from his father. Drop by drop, the library takes its final form, which will eventually be broken apart when someone decides to get rid of it all in one fell swoop upon the death of its owner, giving in to the irresistible urge to erase one's own history or to an economic emergency. To choose is to protect. Neither he nor I could keep the whole collection, but we could choose—imperfectly, with trembling hands—and in so doing, create a new one.

*

My grandfather Juan Manuel made my father and his brother read books that were absurdly difficult for children their age. The way my father told it, if his father handed him Kant, then he had to read Kant. And not only read the book but summarise its contents a few days later. Maybe he was exaggerating the level of difficulty and his father had chosen something lighter like, I don't know, Nietzsche, but that's not the point. These days, it sounds pompous to describe this kind of practice, so much so that my sense of shame begs me to omit this fact. I pause, take a breath, and remind myself that in his memoir, *Oblivion*, Héctor Abad Faciolince makes no bones about recounting things like the different countries he lived in and the countless privileges he enjoyed as a result of being born into his family. In brief: all the cultural capital it's now in poor taste to go through life flaunting. He's not ashamed to be honest and I, as a reader, am grateful for that. So I exhale slowly and repeat to myself that there's nothing to be done about it, this is part of my history, whether I tell it or not.

I find in all this the origin of his insanely high standards. For example, when I was in grade school, my classmates' parents would celebrate their getting an eight on their report cards, whereas I would be scolded as if I'd gotten a three. He always demanded more of me, and I always felt like I was failing. Always feel.

*

I try to take a lesson from personal histories written before and repeat to myself that mine, whatever it may have been, is what it is. If my grandfather was a translator who forced his sons to read philosophy, that's all there is to it. My father was weaned on books. Later, when my grandfather died, he and his brother did the same with their younger sibling, who had been too young to experience his father's cruel lessons. Unsurprisingly, they didn't include my aunt in this mission. My parents were pretty lax with me in this respect, and though I'm sure it would have made me miserable, sometimes I wish they'd imposed such rigorous routines on me. "Go on, kid, read your Heidegger and tell me tomorrow what you understood."

Then I think that what I had instead wasn't so bad: books by Stephen King and J. R. R. Tolkien. They don't offer the prestige of being able to toss out a pretentious phrase here and there, but they did give me many hours of excitement. During the winter I read *The Lord of the Rings* for the first time, I would shower with the book inside a clear plastic bag so I wouldn't have to put it down even for a moment. I never reported back on my readings to anyone, but growing up in a house full of books is a gift for which I'll always be grateful.

*

A few months before his death, they restricted my father's intake of cigarettes and food in order to operate on his treacherous heart. He tried—he made it almost a whole month without smoking. At the end of his life, he returned to fatty quesadillas and cigarettes. I'm so glad he did. It's not God's will to die sick and on a diet. On the other hand, I wonder about his reasons. Was it torture to live with those restrictions? Did he lose all faith in the "long road back to health," as he'd once called it? Or was there something else?

*

An inheritance is also teeth and disease, depression and baldness and hearts that implode. In fact, one's inheritance is often only that. Some people inherit millions; my brother inherited keeping his hair past twenty-five, which is more than my grandfather could say. He, my brother, didn't get anything material because the only thing there was to inherit, the books, didn't interest him. At the same time, we inherited teeth that ache. I got the gift of a pessimism that often builds walls across my path. My father inherited a treacherous heart and the pain of growing up without a father. Family traumas are also, in some ways, a kind of inheritance. Maybe if I start calling them that it will be easier for me to throw them away, as if I were getting rid of an object.

*

One day not so many years ago, my uncle—the one who supported my father the most—said that he, my brother and I should come up with a plan to take care of him in his old age. The phrase that stuck with me like a record skipping in a nightmare, was "Or do you want to see your father living on the street?"

The comment was sparked by the fact that my father was aging prematurely. Suddenly, the energetic man who would run from one side of the Zócalo to the other during a concert, who would carry boxes and boxes of books to literary festivals on his own steam, couldn't stay out of the hospital for two months at a time. He was talking less and less about his work. My uncle's intuition, though melodramatic, proved to be well founded. We didn't know it at the time, but my father was about to become permanently unemployed.

*

Who's going to hire a man in his late fifties with no degree and a health problem?

*

Why all this shame around the body's deterioration? Why is it so taboo to name its aches, its failings? It must have something to do with our phobia of accepting that we are animals in a society that idolises reason as if it were separate from the body, only to realise one fine day that reason is body, and it all begins to atrophy at once.

The humiliation of depending on someone else, of

returning to the lack of autonomy that belongs to infancy and the occasional illness, of realising it's now your only possible future. The terror of losing your quality of life, little by little. Processes most people go through; processes that embarrass us deeply.

In *Winter Journal*, Paul Auster cites Joseph Joubert, who once declared that "the end of life is bitter" and then, at six-ty-one, revised his statement to say: "One must die lovable (if one can)." Auster then goes on to muse, "how difficult it is to be lovable, especially for someone who is old, who is sinking into decrepitude and must be cared for by others. If one can. There is probably no greater human achievement than to be lovable at the end, whether that end is bitter or not. Fouling the deathbed with piss and shit and drool."

Dying well is almost as hard as living well (or more so), though far fewer treatises have been written about it, probably due to complications around assuming someone else's feelings on pain and the body's end. On the other hand, there's the hope that no matter how afflicted one is by aches and pains, the end is not necessarily near.

In Inés Arredondo's story, "The Woman of Shunem," Luisa is sent to care for her uncle Apolonio, who is at death's door. The old man courts her from his deathbed and she eventually gives in to the pressure, thinking he won't last long. But she is mistaken. Uncle Apolonio bounces back, livelier by the day. I've seen an Uncle Apolonio in many ailing people, someone who returns refreshed from the brink. I've seen others who think they'll be like him but instead die suddenly, in a cruel twist of misplaced hope.

My father oscillated between believing he could be healthy again and lovingly caressing the end. On one hand, his phrase about the road back to health; on the other, he wrote "Proof of

Existence," which was basically an obituary. A poem in which he looked back over his entire life. Among those lines is a stanza that makes me tremble each time I think of it. But I'm not ready to read it again, not yet. It was clear that Juan Manuel was feeling his soul leave his body, and also that he didn't want to be a burden on anyone, either out of pride or consideration. I wonder what I would have done if he had decided that he needed a caretaker for the rest of his days and I, as a woman with no offspring, had been the obvious choice. I'm sure he wondered, too.

*

Sacred geezers in hand, it occurs to me that mould is the disease books get. They don't need to be old to suffer from mould or mildew, but those yellow, greenish, black or vermillion stains are more likely to attack as the fibres in their pages weaken. Environmental conditions are also key in the appearance of bookish ailments: too hot or cold, too humid or dry. A bit of sun keeps them healthy because it kills off the lighter spores; too much sun discolours and weakens them. Reading them produces wear and tear but leaving them to gather dust in a stack has different consequences: dust, no matter how fine a layer, traps moisture between the pages and we're back to our first problem.

We often forget that books are, first and foremost, organic matter and that despite their distance from the processes that gave us papyrus and parchment—plant and animal hide, respectively—nature also lies dormant in them. We touch a tree each time we leaf through a book. Plus many chemicals, it's true, and machines, human hands and sometimes plastic, but when all is said and done, it's pulp from the forest. It pains me to think about all the trees that live in my apartment—or die there—but I try to imagine, spurious though this claim might be, that as long as the book exists and remains in use, the verdure wasn't lost in vain but was instead transformed into another form of life.

Books are organisms with a finite history and existence, just like people but longer lived. Also, just like people, if they are cared for, if they are treated at the first sign of illness, they are more likely to remain healthy. Mould is combatted by a bit of sun or, in the worst-case scenario, with alcohol and isolation. Pages that have come unstuck can be glued back in; volumes that have yellowed can be protected from direct sunlight to avoid further damage. So much to do, and so few people doing it. I count myself among that vast population of irresponsible book owners who almost never dust their collections.

*

There is another way to grow old, one in which we don't really take part. Books are sometimes still useful as they age, but sometimes they become words without a foundation, outdated testimonies from another era. They sustain arguments that have come to raise hackles, or which have simply lost value in a given society. It pains me to think how this is true of people, as well. I'm thinking of elderly women unashamed to shout racist slurs that went entirely unquestioned during the first sixty years of their lives. I'm thinking of how anachronic certain things sound, even from the mouths of people well under ninety. So much depends on the listener, as well, but the ideology of a given place and time can develop in ways cruelly opposed to the straight growth of a robust tree. A person ages in body and mind, and unchanging ideas *are aged* by transformations in their surroundings. One process implies movement: the body into illness, the body into its deterioration. The other represents a stasis of the mind within a mobile context.

My father was aging and many of his ideas were aging with him. His body followed its itinerary while his mind doubled down on its cradle-to-the-grave stubbornness. In one episode of *The Simpsons*, the grandfather, Abraham, tells teenage Homer a universal truth: "I used to be with it, but then they changed what 'it' was. Now what I'm with isn't it, and what's 'it' seems weird and scary to me. It'll happen to you." It's frightening to consider how much time we have before the whirlwind of increasingly rapid change relegates us to being with an 'it' that isn't 'it' anymore. How a progressive, nonconforming, defiant man immersed in the principles of '68 could end up on the other side of that spectrum in so many ways. Organic matter and ideas travelling in opposite directions yet, at the same time, reaching the same destination: the passage of time, old age, the book that is at once wise and foolish, mutable and page-stripped. Will I one day be its mirror?

*

I wonder if my father was able to find peace after my grandfather died. Given the terrible circumstances that followed his death, it seems unlikely. A piece of my world was torn away when my father died, but no one pulled the rug I had been standing on from under me. I was able to pay rent the following month; people were generally understanding. My employer gave me time off and support. My family and friends attended the funeral and stayed by my side for a long time. My boyfriend at the time held me through my nocturnal panic attacks, and two wonderful friends helped me and my brother empty my father's apartment, pretending to be literary sommeliers so I could face the great massacre of books sold to the junk dealer. My mother, as always. For all of you, my eternal love and a Pascalised shandy.

My father was left without a father at the age of twelve, which meant extreme financial insecurity, a sudden shift in class and rejection by part of his father's family. I want to pause for a moment to consider what kind of person would add to the pain of a family that had just lost a key member by denying them the security of a home, and why. I wish I could go back in time to that enormous house in Colonia Tacubaya and show that little boy of whom life demanded so much that he could walk a different path. And also punch Marcelino in the face.

*

My grandmother was so strong, to be able to push forward despite everything, to make another home with her three children, one of whom was still very young and another, her daughter, very rebellious. The beauty of life growing around the gaping hole of a death.

*

Now I search among the living for what neither a dead man's memories nor the books in his library can offer. Alfonso tells me that he only saw Pascal cry once. A little while after the divorce, my father lost several teeth. I don't know how many were pulled in total, but a few in the front definitely lost their battle with the dentist. Because it would have been too expensive to get an implant, my father asked for a bridge made of resin. The first time I saw him like that was at a festival in the Zócalo and I still remember the intense distress it caused me.

No one is prepared to watch their parents grow old.

*

It's the contrast with what once was, I think. With the youth that is only fleeting, but which as a daughter you wish were eternal. As a little girl, whenever I didn't go to school my father would take me on his rounds to different newspapers. He wrote columns and reviews for several, which he often signed with pseudonyms other than his habitual one. Juan Villoro described the dynamics at *La Jornada Semanal* in his column-obituary:

> I met Juan Manuel García-Junco in 1995, on one of those hectic mornings at *La Jornada Semanal*, and immediately forgot his name because he preferred to be called H. Pascal. He spoke quickly, in the way of someone who thinks intensely about five things at once. He was an expert in horror and fantasy, adventure novels, comics and science fiction...
>
> Our supplement, *El Curioso Impertinente,* dedicated two pages to stateless works of prose that didn't belong to any specific genre. Pascal could have filled that section on his own, but he waited his turn with patience. Though he was always in a rush to speak, he never complained about our shortcomings and in a way seemed to pity our lack of space.

If the different periods of my father's life were chest x-rays, this one would show a young, strong set of lungs, while the one from his final years would show the twisted knots that are the lungs of a lifelong smoker. In the first x-ray, he was doing what

all the writers in this country do: busting his ass doing twenty
different things, none of which paid much, and starting out
with modest personal projects financed by some institution or
another. By the time the x-ray began to look like an alebrije,
he had completely lost touch with traditional media outlets.

*

He ended up sick and unemployed. By the time he died in
2019, he hadn't had a job since López Obrador took office
in 2018 and my father was dragged along by the current of
layoffs that go along with any new administration. No un-
employment insurance, no savings, no retirement package. I
would look at him and wonder what kind of work a man in
his condition could do; his body was beginning to fail him
and, as a result, his mind was gradually following suit. I imagine he had these thoughts, too, as he explored the labyrinth
of his new physicality. I don't wish it on anyone: feeling your
faculties drop away as if pulled into the underworld by an evil
force intent on stealing your autonomy.

*

Damaged, old, mildewed books don't retire. Their contents,
even when outdated, have value. To me, at least, though this
might not be reflected in economic terms.[18] I'm so glad books

---

18   IN ECONOMIC TERMS: A modern Sisypha, pushing the stone of our
misfortune up a mountain under constant threat of dying squashed under it.

don't have feelings.[19] My father had value, too, though it might not have been reflected in economic terms.

*

The longest-lived books in the library are between seventy and one hundred and forty years old. My grandmother is still alive and is pushing ninety. My grandfather didn't even make it to fifty. My father beat him by a few years and lived to be sixty. Only my grandmother compares to these books in terms of longevity, but she doesn't have the slightest interest in reading them. She doesn't want the sewing machine that had been her grandmother's, then hers, and then mine back anymore, either. She could teach us all a thing or two about surgeries and pain and what it's like to watch the world move from one slap in the face to the next, killing the people you love most. She could teach us all a thing or two about what it means to live in a body that's like a parchment covered with rules stating what you can and cannot do, about limitations and ranges of movement. She could teach us all a thing or two, ultimately, about the desire to keep living despite it all. She is so different from my father. The more I dig into Juan Manuel's personal history, the less certain I am of this last thing: the desire to live. One clue, a key episode, makes me wonder.

---

19   FEELINGS: Sometimes, small reddish insects with no other function than to eat through your torso from the inside out. Other times, pieces of obsidian that refract light.

*

Rainy season, 2018. First call: let's begin. I'm in a meeting at work, around noon, when I see three missed calls from my mother. Strange. I call her back and she says that my father's neighbour found him on the floor, that someone needs to go check on him. She asks me if I can go. I tell her that it will take me a long time to get to Lindavista from la Condesa. She resigns herself: she'll go. She's the only one with keys, after all. Meanwhile, an ambulance is on its way. The neighbour had said something that terrified her: my father is unable to speak.

I try to go back to my meeting, but obviously it's interrupted again. Under the discreet gaze of my colleagues, I get the report from my mother, who is there by now. The paramedic casually tosses out "he had a stroke." My mother repeats the words into the phone and after every syllable I hear an echo that isn't there.

I finish my meeting and have no idea how I get home. I'm scared and wait for the ambulance and my mother to reach Nutrición, the hospital all the way to the south of the city. It's going to take them a long time. I make calls, think about what this means. Our lives are about to change. Will he ever be able to speak again? How long will we need to spoon-feed him? Who will change his diapers?

Nutrición: a hospital with a misleading name where all sorts of maladies are treated. By the time I get there, that night, my brother and his girlfriend are already in the waiting room. My mother has been there for hours; she's wearing the same sweatpants she was in when the emergency overtook her. She hasn't eaten.

The diagnosis is very different from the one that paramedic irresponsibly threw at us.

We can visit my father one at a time. My brother and I head for the waiting area outside his room. We sit down. He steps back out for something and right then a nurse intones "Relative of Juan Manuel García-Junco." He needs someone to help him with his bedpan. I'm all alone, I have no choice.

So I go in. The look in his eyes as he sees me enter is shame. So much shame. That I'm there, that I'm the one who has to help him with his bedpan. That I'm seeing him in such a vulnerable state, covered by just a hospital robe. That he ended up there the way he did, for the reason he did. I set the bedpan under him. He can speak again, but we don't say a word about the situation. Or exchange any loving or comforting phrases. I leave.

Despite the morning's catastrophic prognosis, the unthinkable happens: they discharge him. I hope, with heart in hand, that my brother will return to help him get dressed. Under no circumstances do I want to be the one to do it. I'm sure the feeling is mutual.

In all the chaos, we had forgotten to grab his flip-flops, and since he hadn't been wearing any shoes, they discharge him in socks and pyjamas. The utter vulnerability of shoeless feet waiting for a taxi outside Nutrición. Don't ever, and I mean this literally, don't ever try to hail a taxi outside that hospital. The experience is miserable if you've had a false stroke, and it takes absolutely forever, under any circumstances.

We're going to split up into two cars. I don't say anything, but I hope with every fibre of my being that I don't have to ride in his taxi. I get my wish: my brother and his girlfriend, who turns out to be masterful at dealing with illness, go with him in one car. My mother and I take another. The plan is for my mother to go to my place, where her partner will pick her up; my brother will take my father home. Another relief: my work here is done. But then the plan changes while we're in transit. My father urgently needs to use the bathroom. They're going to have to stop at my apartment, the halfway point. My mother and I arrive long before them. Eventually, the rest of the caravan pulls up. My father needs the bathroom now now now.

A shoeless man walks, docile and a bit sad, with a young couple through an unfamiliar building. They can't find my apartment. They call me. I give instructions, my brother provides points of reference, we don't understand each other. It's all very weird. I go downstairs, we can't find each other. Am I losing my mind?

Mystery solved: they got confused and are in the building next door. We meet outside, on the puddled street and, finally, climb the three high-ceilinged floors to my apartment.

For one ungenerous moment, I wonder if this is a ruse to get inside my apartment. Because it is, indeed, the first time in the three years I've been here that my father has set foot in my living room. He greets my cat—she has, as is her wont, come out to inspect the strangers. He sits for a while; I offer everyone something to eat. He looks around, examining everything: the books, the bookshelves, the decoration. He says it's lovely, I say thank you. His face is the same puffy red canvas it's been for the past several months, though he does manage to smile. In the end, my mother's partner will drop them all off. They live nearby, after all. They leave and I'm suddenly alone.

I'm shaking. I hug my cat.

*

I reach out to everyone I had worried: my father didn't have a stroke—it was, maybe, an overdose of sleeping pills.

FOURTH: THE WORST OF ALL DESERTS

When I hear Alfonso talk about Goliardos, an oft-cited passage from Dickens's *A Tale of Two Cities* tends to rattle around in my head:

> It was the best of times, it was the worst of times, it was the age of wisdom, it was the age of foolishness, it was the epoch of belief, it was the epoch of incredulity, it was the season of Light, it was the season of Darkness, it was the spring of hope, it was the winter of despair, we had everything before us, we had nothing before us, we were all going direct to Heaven, we were all going direct the other way.

By around 2005, Goliardos was at the height of its goliardic glory. Participating in all of Mexico City's book festivals, organising their own science fiction and fantasy festivals every week at El Circo Volador, occasionally bringing writers from other countries to the bigger events they organised in collaboration with universities or public institutions. The texts themselves were selling like hot cakes and the future was full of promise.

The eternal question is: what happened? Why, like a story composed by an unimaginative writer, did it have a beginning and a climax, but no resolution? I thought about writing a history of Goliardos, examining the project through other people's eyes, but their words slid right off me. That wasn't my story. Mine was years of excitement spent at my father's side, and then years of sadness when I forced myself to take distance. It's the story of that enigma: watching it grow and then quietly crumble, never to rise again, without knowing how or why. It's the story, I think, of a shared depression.

Middle school and the first two years of high school corresponded to a period when my father was, at least, excited:

he was more consumed by the growth of his paper baby than that of his flesh and blood offspring or his marriage, but it was also, accidentally, the time when we were closest. I may not have participated in Goliardos, but the project was a milestone in my life.

Creaturas del abismo. Various authors, Colectivo Goliardos, 2004. Anthology coordinated by H. Pascal. Net contents: short stories by 22 authors (predominantly male) and a prologue by an enthusiastic editor of marginalised genres.

"You can call it neo-gothic, cyberpunk or urban legend. It doesn't matter. What matters is the rare ability of these writers to turn the worst of all deserts into their playing field—and they do sometimes play rough." From H. Pascal's prologue to this and all other editions of this collection.

The cover bears an adulteration of one of my favourite paintings when I was a teenager, *The Abduction of Psyche* by William-Adolphe Bouguereau. The classic image of a woman in pure ecstasy, soaring through the heavens in the arms of the god of Love, is crowned in this version by two enormous bat wings emerging from Cupid's back. Behind them, instead of clouds, is a space-scape flecked with brown planets. It's one of my favourite Goliardos collages. My father did almost everything: design, layout, copy-editing. I imagine him spending hours in Photoshop circa 2000, lovingly cropping the borders of the mythological couple until they were perfectly smooth, sizing the bat wings that now keep Cupid aloft. Placing the planets at each corner. I really admire how he designed each chapbook individually, applying his eccentric interpretations of canonical works of art. In 2004, the anthology received the Sizigias

Prize, which the Mexican Association of Science Fiction and Fantasy awarded for a period of just four years. This chapbook, which is in fact a book, is in many ways the culmination of an entire publishing endeavour. I have several editions, including a few with covers printed in colour on heavy-grade cardstock—an exceptional trait for a Goliardo. Inside: some famous names and some not so much. Some of the stories were written in Pascal's workshop and some were written by his friends, whose work he sometimes published without permission. A sample of what Goliardos was, early on.

*

The table of contents is a snapshot of my teenage years, and many of the names listed there belong to people with whom I shared moments that felt like adventures. There was, for example, a girl with long, straight hair who smiled a lot and had recently moved, in a gesture straight out of *The Savage Detectives*, to the Hotel Virreyes, a striking, brusque structure on José María Izazaga that isn't known for being particularly comfortable. Behind its neo-colonial façade, a diverse cast of characters inhabited countless rooms that looked like they hadn't been renovated since the seventies. I found the idea of living in a hotel utterly eccentric, even though the young woman in question wasn't, really. We travelled all around in her car—which my father had commandeered by renaming it the Goliardomobile—packed in like sardines amid chapbooks, stands and other paraphernalia. I don't know how long the Goliardomobile existed, or how long she tolerated the abuse of acting as my father's chauffeur, because my memory is hazy: it neither begins nor ends, it only exists as a group of people in their twenties, a gentleman in his mid-forties and two teenagers—me and my best friend (one of us on the other's lap because we didn't fit)—on our way to more or less decrepit fantasy or science fiction festivals.

That was when I met Alfonso. He'd started out as a biology student with an interest in literature and ended up leaving that degree behind to study Letras Hispánicas. He also put up with my father until the end, despite various disputes and periods of distance. A Pascalised shandy for Alfonso, in recognition of this monumental feat.

*

Something catches my attention as I begin my analysis of this cosmos-covered book. It turns out that my father was an absolute master of the author bio. I read, in *Creatures from the Abyss*:

> Pascal is, essentially, an author of fantasy literature, though he wrote two science fiction novels and a vast array of gothic anthologies. He has also participated in the founding and leadership of two remarkably strange publishing projects: Azoth and Goliardos. The founder and director of two international festivals of fantasy literature based in Mexico City, he is also a kind of goliardic orc, a devious angel who believes, who is certain that life is not a meaning, but rather a desire.

This forces me to reconsider the impossibly dull bios I'm always sending out, the ones in which I try to balance my lack of self-esteem with the rules of the game, which demand a list of achievements that might or might not seem real but need to be included, anyway. What would be my equivalent of "goliardic orc"? Of "devious angel"? I don't know which is worse: including an endless list of publications and awards to prove your worth or inventing ingenious epithets designed to please, hyping your own life like a brand manager.

Special mention goes to the photos that accompanied these bios. In one that appears in the magazine *Replicante*, the foreground is occupied by a hand cooking eggs. Behind this hand is a man with lots of greay hair wearing half a smile and a black t-shirt under a red button-down. In others, his hand is open, blocking the camera. See above regarding the cultivation of the art of insolence, so typically Shandy.

*

> Horror, science fiction, everything understood as fantastic literature, images of other worlds, gritty tales tinged with detective fiction and noir, urban legends—anything that involves peering through the looking glass of the mundane. This anthology does just that: it delivers us into extreme situations and asks us to recognise, to see ourselves in, outlandish characters.

Goliardos' crusade (because that's what it was) was to disseminate genres that, as the prologue also states, didn't tend to be part of "the mainstream, commercially," and could even be considered "marginal." And not only in terms of content: the chapbooks were very inexpensive—even this one, which was more of a book—and were sold in places where books didn't often circulate, like concerts at El Circo Volador or comic book conventions. These events attracted an incredibly diverse population, beyond the fact that most were goths. If one thing can be said for sure, they were not elitist.

A Pascalised shandy for Pascal and company, who managed to create these spaces year after year, against all odds.

The workshops also tried to reach people outside the usual

spectrum: my father led these courses for over thirty years, and they were almost always free. The payment, such as it was, involved supporting Pascal's plans with absolute loyalty or hand-selling chapbooks or organising festival logistics. The workshop description made this perfectly clear:

> More than a workshop, this is a project that encompasses publishing, visual art and sound, that will take place through a variety of actions in different spaces. An experience for really writing, creating and producing published works. For example, participants in the project recently produced the festival *Cosmic Horror: 70 Years After Lovecraft's Death* at El Circo Volador, and published *Beheading the Stars Again, Skinny Devil* and *Sick Angels*, among other titles.

At the time, the situation was clear: Goliardos was what it promised to be—a grassroots publishing project where the people who wrote the texts were the same people who put their work in readers' hands, without any intermediaries. At other times, which was most of them, decisions were made exclusively by Pascal, a benevolent tyrant.

The prologue to *Creatures from the Abyss* indicates that the anthology's content was determined by unusual criteria. It doesn't state what these criteria were, exactly, but I can guess, and the answer seems anything but unusual. He was the sole criterion.

*

Evidence of collective madness. When I was in high school at Prepa 9, it happened more than once that someone came up to me and said that so-and-so wanted to hook up with me because I was Pascal's daughter. I'm not naïve enough to actually believe that was the reason, but even so, the gesture strikes me as odd: why express your attraction to me in terms of your admiration for my father? It would have been enough to say *I want to hook up with her*, but the little cult that Pascal was forming around himself had begun to make its presence known in my world. At El Circo Volador and the Tianguis del Chopo, goths would often come up to us to greet him, their faces lit up with excitement and also, sometimes, lightened with white foundation. My father was basically a jerk, maintaining that delicate balance between distance and brusque charm. It's a rare talent, being able to tell someone to piss off without offending them, no matter how cute you are.

*

There was a time, Alfonso tells me, that Goliardos raked in money at the book fairs. If my father had been a fan of Excel, he would have seen what was obvious to everyone back then: they'd sold thousands and thousands of Goliardos titles in just a few years. For an independent project, it was completely unheard of. Many of the chapbooks piled on my lap right now have an edition printed on them: third, fourth, tenth. They probably reached more readers than any other cultural promotion project in Mexico City's history.

One of the places where the apparently improvised stand appeared most regularly was El Circo Volador, first cousin to the Tianguis Cultural del Chopo. Goliardos sold books at all the venue's events and also organised their own. That period saw the foundation of the Lovecraft Book Club; the price of entry to many Goliardos festivals was "50 pesos, or 25 and the donation of a book of poetry or fantastic literature to the Lovecraft Book Club at El Circo Volador."

*

As Paco Ignacio Taibo II tells it, one day my father invited him to give a talk for his reading group, which I guess was the one at El Circo Volador. This group in particular only read Lovecraft. How strange. When Taibo asked him if he was a big fan of the writer, my father replied that he wasn't, really, but "that wasn't the point." He was there because, after they got through *Cthulhu*, they were going to move on to other things. Lovecraft was the gateway drug. So, when Taibo gave his talk, he took the opportunity to toss in a few thoughts about a guy named Quevedo. Soon after, a bookseller in a nearby Christian bookstore reported record-breaking sales (in other words: sales, period) of Quevedo's sonnets. The customers? "A bunch of goths."

*

Goliardos called itself an association for the defence of cultural rights, that is, for the defence of the right to culture, regardless of a person's background or purchasing power. My father was, in many ways, a great Catholic. He handed out money left and right and offered chapbooks for free to anyone who couldn't pay for them. He was generous, there's no question about that, and he remained true to his socialist vision.

On the other hand, it drove me insane to watch him give so much away when our household was constantly in financial trouble. It must also have been maddening for the people involved in making that money who received almost nothing

116

in return. Or did they? Maybe, like the old volumes on this bookshelf, the value of what they received wasn't economic.

*

I often forget that the name "Goliardos" is, intentionally, destiny. In the Middle Ages, the goliards were itinerant monks who composed and sung poems about drinking, screwing and generally enjoying life. This didn't make them any less Christian, but it did mean they were less accepted by the Church, to the extent that they were frequently condemned at the councils. They lived both within and outside the clergy, the Lord's tightrope walkers. Idle vagabonds dedicated to perceiving the world given to them by God, they wrote some of the period's most memorable poems. At university I read part of *Carmina Burana*, best known for the somewhat cheesy twentieth-century version composed by Carl Orff, and I was struck by how the poems manage to unite joy, doom and humour with critiques of the power held by the sovereigns and, occasionally, satires of the perversions of the Church.

*

In the years after the divorce, El Circo Volador became one of the places I went most often. Contrary to what you might think, not only was I not assigned any tasks to perform, I could also bring a friend, that same best friend, to the concerts there. In exchange for things we would have done just for fun, like hanging posters behind the tables where the chapbooks were stacked, we got to hear Nordic bands and groups from God (or Satan, frequently invoked in that space)-knows-where, while the goliardic horde sold their wares in the lobby. My friend and I, dressed in black and at the height of our adolescence, went to dozens of concerts by bands I'm now embarrassed to name. And that was how we ended up seeing, without knowing who most of them were, groups ranging from semi-Nazi crap to H.I.M. and Lacrimosa, both of which we loved. We also befriended members of the local metal bands that were a fixture at Goliardos festivals. My nights at El Circo Volador were an adventure and an identity, all rolled into one; a safe, happy space.

*

Goliardos was unique in its predilection, which came directly from my father, for poetry within genre fiction. According to my father, the greatest example of this unusual combination was Amado Nervo, who, though not known for this, authored the first Mexican science fiction poem. The issue of Goliardos titled "Amado Nervo: The Last War" concludes like this: "Perhaps, probably, there's no reason to doubt it, Amado Nervo *invented* science fiction poetry." The copy in my hand claims to be the eighth edition, which means that even with their small print runs, Goliardos obviously sold a lot of Amado Nervo.

The workshops my father led in his final years always had poetry in the title; he believed, like many others, that anyone wanting to write prose should read a lot of poetry. This inclination appears in his writing in the form of original, highly polished rhetorical figures.

The last poem in the Amado Nervo chapbook is called "Kalpa" and in this edition is printed in the infernal typeface Comic Sans. It is a short poem about the cyclical nature of time. Following an epigraph from *Thus Spake Zarathustra*,

Amado (to take the liberty of calling him by his first name)
launches headfirst into the ouroboros:

> In all the eternities
> that came before our world,
> who could deny the
> prior existence of planets with their own
> humanities:
> of Homers who
> described the
> first
> heroicities,
> and Shakespeares
> able
> to send the soul into the
> profundities?

I can still faithfully reproduce the way my father recited those
verses, his slightly affected intonation, his eyes fixed on nothing, or on the catalogue in his mind that presented the lines
one after another.

> Serpent
> biting your own tail, inflexible
> circle, black
> ball endlessly
> spinning, monotonous
> refrain of the same
> song, tide of the
> abyss:
> Are you a never-ending story?

*

The list of (overwhelmingly male) authors published by Goliardos in the early years, with or without authorisation, living or dead, on bad terms or not, hated or not, cancelled or not and in no particular order, not even according to how much they are liked by the daughter of Pascal:

Xavier Villaurrutia, Ramón López Velarde, H. P. Lovecraft, Paco Ignacio Taibo II, Juan Hernández Luna, Jessica Freudenthal, Libia Brenda Castro, Christa Faust, Poppy Z. Brite (now Billy Martin), Amado Nervo, Carlos Montemayor, Blanca Martínez, Alberto Chimal, José Luis Ramírez, Juan Villoro, Michelle Morales, Alfonso Franco, José Luis Zárate, Gerardo Horacio Porcayo, Alejandro Rosete Sosa, Manuel Sauceverde, Carlos Rentería, Javier Barriopedro, Cristina Rentería, Gerardo Sifuentes, Ricardo Flores el Abulón (from the band Víctimas del Doctor Cerebro), Arturo J. Flores, Ricardo Guzmán Wolffer, Carlos López, Daniel Nava Quiroz, Fabiola Cantú, José Luis de la O, Marko A. González, Mireli Alcántara *Mili*, Mauricio López, Olash Quintanar, Bernardo Fernández *Bef*, Dolores Zamorano, Eduardo Honey, Elizabeth Soriano, Laura Pírez, Oliver Edén Sánchez, Armando Vega-Gil. A little while later came Andrei Peña *el Señor Santo*, José Luis H. *el Hobbit*, David Enríquez and Eric Ángeles.

A Pascalised shandy for several of them. We won't specify which ones.

*

Much later, at the end, his beloved students: Nadia Mish-ann, Alma Tonatzin Avihe, Karen Lima, Margarita Pacheco, Patricia Bremauntz, Sofi Lara, Stefany Cisneros, Verona

120

Sanmo, Alberta Salamanca, Carmen Lozano, Cessy Mayorga, Jessica Castro, Jessica Robles, Lorena Estrada and Monserrat González. For them, without preambles or reservations, litres and litres of you-know-what.

Of course, most of the chapbooks, especially in the final years, were by the one and only devious angel himself.

*

The prologue to the 2007 edition of *Creatures from the Abyss* includes a brief note regarding the fact that Doris Lessing had won the Nobel Prize that year. It refers to her as a science fiction author, and states that the event is evidence that "we were not wrong... the best part of our creativity begins with the right to imagine." Like Amado Nervo, Lessing is usually described as a realist author, though some of her writing includes elements of genre fiction. The same is true of Kazuo Ishiguro, another Nobel laureate with more than one work of fiction firmly situated in the terrain of the speculative. Italo Calvino's *Cosmicomics* moves between fantasy and science fiction, but he is considered an author of capital-L Literature through and through.

My favourite example of this is Kurt Vonnegut, who regularly plays with the existence or fiction of aliens in the lives of his protagonists. Kilgore Trout, one of his recurring characters, writes dime-store science fiction novels and walks the fine line between hallucination and foreshadowing, between abject failure and saving the universe. Just like Daniel Quinn from Paul Auster's *New York Trilogy*, who writes successful crime novels under the pen name William Wilson, Kilgore Trout seems to suggest that a serious writer cannot and should not dedicate their energy to certain genres. It's always a good idea to have a marginal, remorseful character on hand who embodies the author's deepest fears and shows what could happen if they get too close to the edge. Any day now, I'll create one of my own.

Both Auster's and Vonnegut's writing borders on genre fiction, but they usually escape by means of metafictional elements that mock the genres themselves. Ishiguro, Calvino and Lessing, on the other hand, have written within the limits of speculative literature but for some mysterious reason are not included in its canon.

It has been said that genre is just a tool used by the publishing industry, but it's also used in the academic intellectualisation of literature. This is changing, but it's still hard to think about science fiction as Literature with a capital L, and the same goes for detective fiction and fantasy. Goliardos insisted on moving between these genres at a time when they were even less accepted, and repeatedly managed to demonstrate a level of interest in them that many people seemed eager to ignore.

The problem is that Pascal began to see himself as the vanguard of the marginal—or, as Alfonso says, he began to present himself as The Great Loser.

*

My father went with me to the Tianguis Cultural del Chopo to buy my first pair of heavy metal boots. I can attest that they weighed nearly three kilos each and were, he would say, ugly as sin. On that same trip, I bought a pair of black and red striped leggings and a studded belt, also unbelievably heavy. When my mother saw me in the whole outfit, topped off by a black mini-skirt and my few "extra kilos," all she said was, "You get more exotic every day, don't you, honey." That trip to the Chopo for my *darks* look was probably accompanied by the standard distribution of flyers for some poetry festival and encounters with characters in varying degrees of velvet.

*

Now I learn something that adds a touch of bile to the story. With a smile on his face, Alfonso tells me about one time, after a festival that was half in Tlaxcala and half in Mexico City where the Goliardos had sold like hot cakes, "Your father skipped out, leaving me and Michel at the Museum of Mexico City like, 'see you in Tlaxcala, suckers.' We hadn't eaten all day; we hadn't even had a minute to rest. He took all the money, and it's not like we were going to be able to sell any more." They eventually made it there by bus, with some tortas that another illustrious member of Mexico's movement for marginalised genres, Libia Brenda Castro, had given them, and which seemed like the most delicious sandwiches on earth at the time. Why did they put up with him? A benevolent tyrant.

Then something else. I'm told that Paloma Saiz, who has been the director of the Freedom to Read Brigade for some time now, and my father were always at each other's throats, but that she kept letting him set up his stand at her project's book fairs because he was one of the few people who really did create new readerships. In his obituary, Villoro adds: "Many people started reading because of what he put in their hands. An unrelenting proselytiser, he held forth about elves in the Metro and the language of dragons in the Zócalo. His was an imagination without hierarchies, open to all stimuli."

The yin and yang of promoting culture.

*

My father unintentionally inserted himself into a tradition of travelling books, of those encyclopaedia sales reps who went door to door with their leather-bound volumes—his were just made of bond paper in two colours. An heir not to the refined traffickers of rare books, but rather to the wagon brimming with used copies on their way to anyone looking to read them and, even more, to people about to discover a book based on the words of an expert orator, though they may not know it yet. Portable literature, I've said it before.

For a long time, access to books depended on the complex trajectories of adventurers and outcasts. In Christopher Morely's *Parnassus on Wheels*, a man travels by mule-drawn cart through rural areas of the United States in the early twentieth century. When he stops in a town and pulls back the cloth covering his wares, it turns out that he isn't selling cure-all potions or other talismans: his display contains books. With the voice of a great salesman, the protagonist Mifflin espouses the virtues of his product before the sceptical gaze of the town's inhabitants. Irene Vallejo's book, which includes this reference, describes the vicissitudes of book ownership throughout history. The idea that it might be impossible to obtain books is pretty much unthinkable to us middle-class urbanites. One could argue that an internet connection and a screen is all you need to access countless works in digital format, expanding the possibilities even further.

The problem is much more complex. Access to books, as seen in *Parnassus on Wheels*, also has to do with a mindset. Growing up in an environment where books are valued and accessible leads to the reproduction of those conditions, whereas the opposite tends to limit the possibility of desiring them.

Beyond the question, which seems an important one to ask, of why everyone is supposed to want access to books and why our idea of culture is orientated towards things that can be included in them, reading advocacy tends to lose sight of this crucial point. As Irene Vallejo argues:

> Mifflin discovers that the deeper into the countryside he goes, the fewer books are to be seen and the worse those he does find are. With his singular eloquence, he proclaims that it would take an army of booksellers like him, willing to visit workers in person, tell their children stories, speak to the teachers in their tiny schools, and put pressure on the editors of agricultural magazines until books circulate through the country's veins and the holy grail reaches the remote farms of Maine.

Books are expensive and seem irrelevant when set against the struggle to survive, a context of extreme violence or ridiculously long workdays that make it impossible to have a life outside. The deep fatigue that comes from being exploited doesn't leave much space or desire for reading, either.

One of Pascal's central tenets was that writers work for the reading public. No one is obligated to read what you write, and there's no one to blame but yourself if people ignore your texts. Based on this premise, he fashioned himself into one of the best salesmen I have ever seen in action. From his station at the Goliardos stand, he could sell a chapbook to anyone. He would ask any unsuspecting individual who paused to take a peek what they liked to read, and suddenly there he was with four books under his arm, plus one more as a gift. This approach sometimes even worked when the person answered that they didn't enjoy reading anything at all.

You have to imagine him describing the work of Horacio

Quiroga as "post-rural gothic with slaughtered chickens" to a hapless teenager who braved leaning his pimply face over the cover images of punk vampire chicks or collections of "kickass *darks* poetry" while a thirty-year-old goth ran her eyes over a Goliardos edition of Villaurrutia.

This was the source of at least part of the success of his nomadic library. For a shy teenager like me, his salesmanship was beyond the pale and just watching him made me uncomfortable.

*

One of these nomadic pieces is in my hands right now, fresh from the shelves. I ask the reader of these lines to bear with me through the shock of what they are about to see. This poetry chapbook is called: "iN tHe LiKwiD pUpiL oF thE well." Just like that. Dysorthographic discourse—that was what my father called this orgy of upper and lower case letters in order to "elevate" it. At the dawn of the social media and smartphone era, writing was modified to communicate efficiently. Highbrow individuals and the lowest of lowbrow television shows were equally vocal in criticising the horrific linguistic degradation represented by the use of "U" instead of writing out "you" and the ominous omission of vowels. Writing like that was a way to connect with the most pedestrian, least literary, forms of expression. Pascal, an ally to all marginal causes, decided this was an ideal space for experimentation and wrote a couple of poetry collections in dysorthographic discourse. He talks about this choice in a video from not so long ago, before killing the whole thing with one phrase: "But then I'd forget to put in the spelling mistakes and couldn't be bothered so now I try just to write normally."

In a way, inclusive language is similar to this deliberate attempt to shake up academic rules, to generate static in the unexamined consensus and attempt to represent a new reality. In the case of social media, a popular and oral form of writing rejects the rules of writing "correctly" and focuses on what is necessary in that specific context. In the case of inclusive language, a clear attack on writing and speech reveals new realities: the importance of women's visibility in language and the expansion of non-binary identities. They are similar, but with an enormous difference: inclusive language is planned, whereas the language of social media is spontaneous. Nonetheless, when my father used the latter deliberately, he turned dysorthographic discourse into a rhetorical, political and aesthetic proposition. Without meaning to, he set in motion something like what would happen with the gender-neutral language he found so jarring, the language I now use to write this book about him. In a way, I'm doing the same thing he did, with just as uncertain an outcome. Life's little mysteries.

*

In one of the chapbooks, I catch sight again of a phrase that has come to seem like a prayer: "Life is a desire, not a meaning."

*

Creatures from the Abyss was actually titled *Creatures from the Abyss 1*. The number indicates that it was meant to be part of a series. But 2 never came, much less 3, despite the fact that Goliardos existed, nominally at least, until my father's death over a decade later. This lack of continuity is evidence of a rupture among the group. A rupture so massive that the project went from being a collective, as it still describes itself in this chapbook, to being an insolvent business run by a benevolent dictator. A rupture largely caused, according to Alfonso, by my father's greatest talent: his capacity for self-sabotage.

*

Alfonso tells me that his theory of The Great Loser came in part from my father's favourite book, *Spartacus* by Howard Fast. An enslaved man named Spartacus rebels against his cruel Roman masters and becomes an iconic figure of the struggle against injustice that he ultimately does not overcome, though he dies a hero in the most critical battle of all. History will elevate him, though his fight would appear fruitless. The Great Loser wins in losing because his defeat reveals the others to be wrong.

"But we could have won," says Alfonso.

*

I think the theory of The Great Loser explains the symptom of a broader disease—a disease born the day my grandfather had a heart attack and unwillingly abandoned his family, and then made worse by machismo, which I do see as one of the major clefts that ended up splitting my father open, leading to the night when his heart stopped behind a sweet smile and a book resting on his belly.

FIFTH: IN THE BEGINNING WAS THE WORD

In the beginning was the word adorned with feathers, the calm and happy voice, the gift of literature distilled through a dark moustache and a thick beard on each of the thousand and one nights of my childhood. In the beginning was a father who hugged with his whole body at the drop of a hat, a playful father who could make anyone smile with his wit. Able to make anyone smile, but especially his daughter. In the beginning was waiting for him to come home every night to see what gift he'd picked up along the way. In the beginning were afternoons in Cocoyoc building haunted castles out of toilet paper rolls. The little worlds that were ours alone and our games. Above all, in the beginning was Tolkien, *The Worst Witch*, *The Hounds of the Morrigan*, *The Last Dragon*, flying ferrets, magic dreams, rusty armour, worlds better and worse than this one. In the beginning was a daughter and a father who loved each other very much.

Later, there were many other things.

There is a ghost book in my father's library. Mine. The card should read: *Antikythera: Toothed Mechanism*, 2018, Fondo Editorial Tierra Adentro. Net contents: my first novel. *For Angélica and Manuel.*

I sent my father a copy through my mother, unsigned. Just one of the hundred my publisher had sent to me. She might even have needed to suggest it. A few weeks later, my father gave it to my grandmother. "I'll get another one from you." I don't know if the rules of this project allow me to base a chapter on a book that's not in the collection. Forgive me, Oulipo. But it's a ghost that's very present because I never got the chance to give him another copy. He died a few weeks after the book came out.

*

I often wished that my father had stuck to his wool blazer with elbow patches, that he had inhabited the cliché I saw all around me in "successful"[20] men of his generation as I began to spend more time in literary circles.

This desire was united with my longing for a father I could introduce to my friends without worrying what they were going to think of his mullet, his faded pants and his eternal sneakers begging for retirement. A father who wouldn't start giving out weird chapbooks with naked women all over them at the drop of a hat. It was to my advantage that almost no one but those closest to me could connect us. Because his real name was a mystery.

My admiration for the figure went hand in hand with all this. Pascal, the gentleman who, dressed in colourful shirts, organised festivals populated by goth and metalhead shadows. The one you'd always find at every book fair, the one who greeted everyone he saw and almost always received an enthusiastic response. The one who would stroll around with his students, demanding discounts for the books he bought them and reciting poetry from memory. There and only there, in his world, which hadn't yet become mine, was I proud when he introduced me as his daughter.

---

20   SUCCESSFUL: What is life? Madness. What is life? An illusion, a shadow, a fiction. And our greatest good is but small, for all of life is a dream, and dreams themselves are only dreams.

In 2006, when I was seventeen, I sent him a story and asked for his opinion. It seems pretty awful to me now, but at the time it was the only thing I had written in years, probably since childhood. It had been his fault that I'd stopped writing, as I'll explain later. He never responded. What he did instead was publish the story in a Goliardos chapbook titled *Beheading the Stars Again: New Fantasy from Mexico*, without asking my permission or, for that matter, informing me. A surprise gift. One I discovered while leafing through the little volume, the cover of which features a woman against a pink background opening her mouth like a black hole. (In ecstasy, or is she dead?) I held onto this chapbook all these years, and now it's (re)united with the ones I brought from his apartment. It's a bit creased but in good condition, aside from that. On the first page, right below the title, is a note I'm ashamed to transcribe, but for the sake of documenting the passage of time, here they are: "To my main squeeze, from Aura (even though you only pretended to like my story). January 31, 2007 In Extremo." On the following page are written, in lipstick, the words: "I love you. 1 year and 4 months." The part about In Extremo refers to the concert, at El Circo Volador of course, during which this offering was made. O horrors of teenage love. The question is: how did a gift for my high school boyfriend end up back in my hands? It's not the first time this has happened to me—nor, do I imagine, will it be the last. In this case, however, it's the only copy I have of the chapbook, which bears on its first page a quote from Vladimir Mayakovsky that I love despite having no clue what it means.

Look—

they have again beheaded the stars,
the sky is red with the blood of slaughter!

These lines are followed by the statement that appears in all the Goliardos: made and printed in Mexico. An independent publication.

Independent, human, generous. The best thing about self-publication is that you can do whatever you want, even publish your own daughter. The worst thing is that it will never be considered entirely serious or important. You can set your hopes on your work becoming, years later, cult classics like certain pulp novels from the last century did, but nothing guarantees that the next beheading of stars won't snuff out your lovingly designed publications. The disadvantages of portable literature.

*

My father studied psychology at the Xochimilco campus of the Autonomous University of Mexico. In his last semester, with only one course remaining, he developed appendicitis. He turned in his final paper, "which was excellent"[21] a day or two after the deadline. His professor showed no mercy: he refused to accept it. At that point, Juan Manuel weighed his options and decided to walk away.

At least, that's how he always told the story of why he never got his degree. My mother, meanwhile, completed the same programme and began practicing as a psychologist at a preschool that was part of the National Polytechnic Institute,

---

21   EXCELLENT: But who's looking at whom from the depths of the sky?

the same CENDI where I would later spend my infancy. After that, when my brother was ten and I was fourteen, she got her master's degree in a programme conducted partially online that inflicted on her countless technological hardships. My mother worked at the Poly in different roles until her retirement a few years ago. She experienced the stability of yore with a tenured position and all the benefits that go with it. A Pascalised shandy for her, and make it a double.

My father said he didn't care about not having a degree. Alfonso tells me that this was, in fact, one of his greatest obstacles. Not even all the cultural capital he hauled around could offset the absence of that little piece of paper.

*

Since the rise of public education, the university has become a kind of benevolent tyrant. What monopolised it? The administration of competence, of knowledge. You might know more than the shrewdest lawyer, but without a document with your name and the seal of some institution or another, it won't do you much good. We live in a world where the only legitimate and authorised knowledge comes at the end of a process of social alchemy: the institutional seal that changes a simple piece of paper into a degree.

I find the inflexibility of the professional sphere completely ridiculous. If my father had finished his degree in medicine—a programme he started and abandoned before psychology—he could very easily have taught a literature course at the university, for example. In one sense, the existence of your degree is more important than what that degree is in. It might be excessive to say that not having a degree is a prison sentence, but it most certainly is an obstacle. He, who knew much more about literature than most graduates of the PhD programme; he, who had read incessantly since childhood and knew thousands of poems by heart. He, who had been teaching for ten years, was—according to the system—unqualified to teach.

School is the vessel that contains the hypocritical dream of education as the cornerstone of democracy, when in reality it democratises few things, homogenises many and exacerbates the obstacles facing those who were already at a disadvantage. In any case, it's a necessary evil. Before the public system was created, a person's education depended on their family's resources. This meant that a certain kind of knowledge was only within reach of a social class that could afford the luxury of sending its little blessings to school or of hiring private tutors. Public education broadened the reach of something that had been the exclusive purview of the bourgeoisie.

But this doesn't mean that other forms of education, the kind that don't follow a curriculum organised by fields of study, aren't an education—only that, according to the hierarchies of the world we live in, a certain type of knowledge is valued more highly than others. I'm sure that somewhere on the planet there's a brilliant physicist who can see folds in galaxies[22] but can't manage to prepare a quesadilla.

My father's case was one of extremes. A man with an enviable education gained outside the classroom but no paper to back it up, and a stubborn drive to embody the margins. At one point, already wedded to this idea, he began calling other writers (always men) *mainstreamers* in order to distinguish himself from them. Maybe in his arrogance he even thought, in his most refined French, that the university could take its

---

22   GALAXIES: Blood on the horses of the mOoN, but hOo the heLL sed the eaRtH is rouNd, anyway?

degree "and shove it," because the rules and regulations of the Mexican state were no match for him and his many qualities. He was going to prove he could do things his own way. Be careful what you wish for.

*

I see his books lined up on the shelf. I examine them slowly, feeling my way. There are at least six novels: a space opera titled *Fire for the Gods*, two works of historical erotica—*The Executioner's Tears* and *The Dragon's Tongue*—a historical novel, *The Grail's Magic*, and an Inuit fable, *The Song of Ice*. Many poetry collections. A few stories scattered here and there among chapbooks and other volumes. I see many years of writing, many storms of unexpected beauty, many forlorn hours when it wouldn't come together. The elegance and precision of his often-poetic prose is apparent even in his lewdest moments. I imagine my father typing away in my childhood home, first in what was the spare room before my brother was born—on one of the first laptops that were widely available—and later in the middle of the living room, where the desktop ended up and would remain until he moved out. I see him writing all the ever-loving day long, never needing to steal time from the night because he never had a conventional job that would require regular hours (a fact that cost him dearly at many points in his life, though not so dearly as it cost my mother, who was the only one with a stable income). I see him printing on his inkjet, cutting out pages. Assembling books with all-purpose glue and card stock for the covers. I was always amazed at how much they seemed like real books. That sense of wonder and mystery, which I felt for many years—before it turned into imbalance, freefall and then just plain apathy—was surely what set me on the path to being a writer.

I had a strong start. My career as a mini literata really took off. When I was seven, I harnessed my newly acquired ability to string letters together and debuted with a short story. I don't remember what it was about, but I do remember that I read it while we ate quesadillas at the dining room table, which was too big for our small apartment.

A resounding success with the audience, which consisted of my parents and tiny brother.

But then—as with Icarus when he flew too close to the sun—came the fall. After sampling the sweet taste of praise, I doubled down for my next piece. My memory of this second story is clearer because it was forged by trauma. The protagonist was Winnie the Pooh, and there was an army of cockroaches, probably his nemesis. To recreate the conditions of my first performance, I read while my audience ate quesadillas. Deathly silence. My father criticised it harshly: he didn't like Winnie's role in the story. He applied the logic of a writing workshop to a seven-year-old girl and—who would have thought?—the only result was sending me into a state of creative paralysis that would last approximately ten years.

How strange that I've always had a reputation for being a bit rough in writing workshops. And how strange that, had no one told me, I would never have realised it. I guess that kind of thing seems totally normal if you grew up with it in every aspect of your life. This, too, is an inheritance.

My great-grandfather was tough to the point of neurosis, my grandfather made young children read books well beyond their level and my father was one of the cruellest critics I've ever had the misfortune of witnessing in action. What does that make me?

*

If he behaved that way with his daughter, it's easy to imagine how he was with everyone else. My internet research offers ample evidence of his sadistic approach. This text by Arturo J. Flores, one of the students closest to him, describes that first season of the Goliardos workshop-but-not-only-workshop far better than I could:

> ... he knew how to bring a bunch of freaks and outsiders who dreamed about becoming writers into the fold and how to teach us... At five minutes to five we'd accompany Pascal—in his habitual attire of checked shirt and jeans, with his white alchemist's beard and his cigarette clenched between his teeth like Clint Eastwood in *The Good, the Bad, and the Ugly*—to get his americano at [Café] Trevi...
>
> For the next two hours, the Goliardos would read our bad prose and worse poetry. We battered one another mercilessly with our critiques. We pissed all over each other's texts. Not everyone could take it. We watched several people step into the Goliardos dojo and slink out with their tail between their legs, never to return. On the other hand, many of us published books, won prizes and even earned a few pesos with our writing.
>
> But H. Pascal never relented. He was always the cruellest among us, the most callous and crude in his comments. He liked to watch us pick ourselves up off the floor, wipe away the blood and keep fighting.

My father's love of violence can be glimpsed between the lines above, and also in a phrase he tossed at Arturo while he read: "You're an alcoholic for clichés."

My father's victims varied. The few times I went to his workshop, I saw one retiree or another who had dropped in looking for a nice way to spend her time leave with a new trauma caused by the boorish comments of the workshop leader with his, shall we say, lack of subtlety. My recent inquiries have led me to similar stories that took place outside the workshop. An example: Israel Ramírez, a.k.a. Belafonte Sensacional, used to work in the ministry of culture, where my father spent some of his best years under the leadership of Alejandro Aura, another dear friend who has since passed away. Israel told me that he had been fascinated by my father's public figure, so he kept trying to approach him, even though he didn't know if my father liked him at all. (See above: performance of arrogance.) Once, on what appears to have been a masochistic suicide mission, he dropped a few of his poems off in my father's office to see what he thought. When he returned for them, my father tossed one of his famously cutting remarks at him: "Some people just don't know what poetry is." Israel and I were at a party when he told me this story, and despite the loud music and his easygoing tone, my face fell with shame. I needed to seek shelter in the mantra I repeat to myself any time someone, with or without malice, recounts some atrocity committed by the elder goliard.

Repeat: you are not your father; you are not responsible for his sins.

While I was busy reciting mantras and drafting an indirect apology, Israel snapped me out of my trance by telling me that my father's brutality had done him good because after that he'd "started writing differently."

Namaste and another mantra.

Repeat: not everyone feels the way you do; not everyone saw him the way you did.

*

I repeat my mantras often: when it comes to anything related to money, any time someone approaches me to say that my father still owes this person or that one and even more that bleak day when a notice was delivered to my mother's house that the ministry of revenue was going to perform an audit, who knows why. I hope I never find out.

A literary inheritance can also mean inheriting precarity or a fear of falling into the void. Brigitte Vasallo talks about the indelible scar of growing up in poverty—even if life ends up smiling upon you later, it remains in the form of a vague fear that everything will vanish from one day to the next, or (and especially) that you're insufficient, an interloper. And many other fears that begin in the cradle.

For as long as I can remember, I watched my father fight to earn a living and barely manage to scrape by. I remember my uncle the economist explaining how my father worked a lot but only in jobs that paid badly, which was just bad business; I remember my mother growing more and more frustrated because she was the only stable source of income. I remember my brother complaining that they'd forgotten to pay his tuition for lower school. And me, thinking of my aspirations for my own education, I never understood why we never had enough money. Most of all, I remember him searching and searching and searching for different ways to get money, each of which ended up like a house of cards.

When I decided to study literature, I embarked on my path convinced that I would never have a cent to my name. I accepted it as an incontrovertible truth and repeated it to anyone who would listen: just assume you won't live well. The first thing I did when I became a writer was panic about my future and get myself a "real" job. The second thing I did was write. Recently, I've switched the order, but the elements remain the same. At the end of the day, my family life was an eternal struggle because my father never brought enough money home.

*

I run my eyes over the wealth of books that surround me in my middle-class apartment—and, earlier, that surrounded my father in the middle-class apartment where he lived, owing three months of rent—and think about how much has changed in order for me to have these objects around, despite everything.

My father would go to used bookstores and buy entire stacks of the same title. If Lope de Vega was on sale, he'd grab five copies and give them all away. The poetry published by Lumen on the middle shelf is living proof of this. Multiple copies of the same book, books he gave to me and that I watched him give to others. I myself have chosen to do the same with some of them. I give them to people I really care about, making sure to explain why they smell like cigarette smoke. I wonder about this obsession with buying so many books to give away; I wonder if everyone who loves books will end up like that. From what I've seen, I'm inclined to see it as one of his idiosyncrasies. After all, as we saw when we emptied his apartment, he did have the spirit of a hoarder.

Sometimes I think that growing up with the wound of his father's sudden death and under such difficult financial circumstances created in him the sensation that misfortune could strike at any time. So it was probably best to have multiples of everything. Why have one reusable shopping bag when you could have thirty and use them as many different ways as your imagination allows? Why buy just one roll of packing tape when twenty-four fit inside a plastic storage container? One packet of tuna? Better make it ten. Why have just one copy of a book when you can have three and be ready in case you need to give one away? These things were his inheritance.

*

As I look at "The Green Room," the story of mine he published in 2007, it occurs to me that my father gave me the gift of my first publication, and I didn't realise it at the time. In part, because I wasn't sure that appearing in a Goliardos anthology edited by him really counted. I was so used to seeing them everywhere that I never understood how many people wanted to appear in those little sui generis volumes. Nor did I understand that it meant other people could read my words, the miracle of that. Only now, too late of course, am I able to say thank you.

*

A few years before that publication, when I was thirteen, my father gave me a different gift: a story that explained why my name is Aura. In the volatile days of paper, he printed it in purple ink. It was, I remember, a bit ethereal, like "your mother and I were searching for a name that felt like a breath, a name that would caress." And that's the etymology of my name: aura-ae, Latin, meaning gentle breeze. This story contradicted the somewhat more mundane explanation my mother once offered me: that I was named Aura because they saw the name in a novel by Carlos Fuentes and they liked it. Literature tells big, beautiful truths halfway, and both versions are almost certainly accurate. I kept the print-out taped to the wall of my room for many years, finally convinced there was value to having a writer for a father. The text also taught me something else. A while later, someone asked why I was named Aura and I found myself incapable of paraphrasing and fell back on the laconic, "because of Carlos Fuentes." It was impossible to convey the content of my father's story without reproducing its form. The greatest gift was learning that words don't only transmit ideas, they also transmit themselves.

*

The book I never signed for him, my first novel, was written when he and I had pretty much stopped speaking. I left home at twenty-one and moved from the remote lands of Gustavo A. Madero, all the way to the north of Mexico City, to the triply aspirational Colonia Del Valle, followed by the slightly-more-relaxed Colonia Narvarte. I'd always wanted to leave the G.A.M., as it was known by its daughters, because it was far away and because its trees, except in a few exceptional places, were an optional accessory. I needed to run as far as I could from that place, which held so many painful memories. My father still lived there. After the divorce, he found an apartment nearby—according to him, for the sake of me and my brother. I got out of there as fast as I could. If we'd seen each other rarely before that, afterwards it became a true rarity.

For several years, not too long before his death, my father and I would meet from time to time outside the Eugenia metro station, near where I lived and where he went, sporadically, to the office where he held his last job. He didn't have much money, but he would give me single-serving packets of tuna and books—usually published by a government initiative—each with a low-denomination bill hidden some-where among their pages. Whatever new chapbook he might have published would often make an appearance in our fleet-ing and uncomfortable encounters on a yellow bench outside the metro station, surrounded by the racket of the avenue and the smell of street food. Ah, nostalgia.

*

We are our memories, but when something like a dead man moves far into the past, those memories begin to feel like in-truders. After all, the well from which they spring has dried up. Where's that water coming from, then? Maybe that's why so many people choose to live inside those remembrances and forget about the here and now. They build a monument to the past, which they don't want to sully with any coarse intrusion from the present.

On this lazy Sunday afternoon, I wonder if I'm not doing the exact same thing by refusing to consider these bookshelves mine, despite all evidence to the contrary. They're a kind of time machine. I suddenly recall the notion that if a space trav-eller were to dare change something in another time, no matter how minor, her act would spark tremendous consequence in the future. Something in my mind keeps insisting that insert-ing one of my books among his would destroy everything.

To overcome this resistance, I imagine mixing all the books I had before with all the books that were his. There are many theories about the best way to organise a library—as many as there are heads. The idea of using the alphabet was a contribution from the sages of Alexandria, who faced increas-ing organisational challenges as the number of texts in their holdings grew harder and harder to grasp. Callimachus was the first to classify literature by genre. When we talk about organising libraries, we often talk about Aby Warburg and his "law of the good neighbour," according to which the search for any book should lead you to pick up the one right beside it. Unfortunately, none of these theories considers the, shall we say, sentimental aspect of this question. Not even the law of the good neighbour—which bears a resemblance to the mysticism I've employed thus far when navigating this library, a mix of intuition and rationality—explains what to do with a collection that is, for its owner, pure emotion.

I had my first attack of librarian-itis when I was still a little girl. On index cards I found lying around the house, I registered the names of each and every book in my room, which at that time were in one of the bookshelves that came from my father's apartment. If memory serves, each card corresponded to a section of that wooden behemoth, and the cards were organised thematically. Every so often, I would dedicate an entire day of those delicious weekends when there's nothing at all to do,[23] to coming up with a new order and later mending the chaos that inevitably struck. Now that I have shelves and shelves of books, it's been years since the last time I tried to organise them. This might be the moment to start, or at least to take inventory, create a map of my own for navigating the volumes and coming to really know them. Lists are always a balm for anxiety.

Sometimes I imagine a parallel universe where, instead of selling part of my father's collection to the junk dealer, I had kept all his books and was giving them away one by one, or

---

23 NOTHING TO DO: A concept that dies in adulthood, at which point you always having something that you *could* be doing, though you could also not be doing it—and, as a result, you never truly have leisure time.

even just dropping them in interesting places. At the very least, I could have made a catalogue and thereby conferred on them the status of a collection. Irene Vallejo says that every collector needs an inventory, for reasons that seem obvious to me now:

> The things they strive to gather might be scattered again one day, perhaps sold or plundered, leaving no trace of the passion and expertise that galvanised their previous owner. It's painful for even the most modest collector of stamps, books or records to imagine that in the future, those items chosen one by one and for highly personal reasons will return to the tangle and disarray of the thrift store. Only in its catalogue can the collection survive its own wreckage; this is the proof that it existed as a whole, as a painstaking plan and as a work of art.

I might not have been able to catalogue the original collection, but at least I can do it with what I have on hand and eventually unite that with my own books. That would be the definitive collection. I might not have done it then, but I'll do it now; I'll replicate the system of index cards for the books on the shelves now, just like I did when I was a little girl. That way, I can add more over time and they won't be invaders, but rather new inhabitants. Just not yet.

*

Then I think, in a clearly sophistic manoeuvre, that this book, too—my first book, which I'm slipping now into his bookshelf, a wily stowaway—is also part of my inheritance. The inheritance of literature, which, though it didn't come only from him, does owe much to him.

I see my *Antikythera* among the women writers who

inhabit his bookshelves, and I find it hard to believe that I'm in the same league. And yet, my book was baptised just like any other in this small but spirited world that is (mainstream or whatever we want to call it) literature: with a presentation. When I was little, my parents would go to the presentation of one of my father's books and I would stay awake imagining scenarios on the level of a mysterious event at a palace. And while book presentations are certainly not what my Tolkien- and Calvino-inflected imagination made them out to be, there is, I would argue, something magic about them.

Only someone who has experienced their very first book presentation knows that stabbing nervousness: it's that party you thought no one would attend and your comprehensive exams, all rolled up in one. My father showed up at mine in the same faded black jeans as always, the Crocs that had become the only shoes that could accommodate his swollen feet, his bright checked shirt and the sickly appearance of his final years. He chose a seat far from the stage where the presenters would be, close to the door. There was no way he could see anything from there, but he refused to move forwards. He never liked being in the first row, and I have to admit that the sofa he'd occupied was much more comfortable than the plastic chairs lined up in front of the stage. In any case, it made me sad to see him like that, sick and ungainly with white splotches of talcum powder on his clothing, with his hacking cough.

The presentation went like all book presentations do. Among friends, family and anyone else who wanted to be there, my book was ritually born. At the end, my father stood and came up with two of his students to say hello. He'd been promoting the event on social media and had invited several of them personally. He wanted the event to be a success. With a smile and a cheerful wisp of a voice he introduced me to the two women and congratulated me. He ran into another of his students, someone I knew who hadn't been to his workshop in a long time, and she promised she'd start going again soon. Then my father drew close to me, despite my best attempts to repel him, and said, almost whispering into my ear, that my novel was "something Borges would have written, if he had written science fiction."

The blurred photos he took that day are his fallible, proud eyes: the back of my head as I sign a book. A picture taken from all the way in the back, in which the audience looks crooked and strange and a pillar blocks part of the view. Another of me from behind, with my hunched back right in the foreground, then one of me smiling while I speak. The photos dance on the Goliardos Facebook page; they move like his heavy gait as he crossed the bookstore, clicking away with his telephone, bearing the afflicted corporality of the man holding the camera. He sees me and smiles; he sees me and feels proud, he sees me and he sees that first draft I sent him, the only one, on December 21, 2014—the draft that he'd said, with his characteristic harshness, lacked narrative arcs and who knows what else; the text I never sent him again. I close my browser.

*

"The novel Borges would have written if he had written science fiction." I've never been good at taking compliments, much less compliments like that one, so I did what I do best: I reacted badly. I replied, coldly, that my novel wasn't science fiction. How did that make him feel? In any event, his smile never faded.

All those blurry photos taken from strange angles that were his specialty will live on in the enduring memory of that social network. What's missing from these myriad photographic records and those taken by others is him. The only witness to his presence is his gaze, clouded with emotion. The missing photo is of us.

I slide my book into the bookshelf.

SIXTH: THE LOSING BATTLE

I need to get my head above water for a while. I pull one book after another from the shelf, looking for signs of past readings, for marks that speak to me of Juan Manuel before the blurred gaze of his photos at my book presentation.

Alexis o el tratado del inútil combate by Marguerite Yourcenar, Alfaguara (the oldies). Net contents: a confessional letter that Alexis sends to his wife to announce the end of their marriage.

"My friend, we believe for no reason that life transforms us: what it does is wear us down, and what it wears down in us are the things we learn."

In my increasingly rapid exploration of the books in this library, I have come across few with more underlining throughout than *Alexis*. A faint pencil traces a square around the number of many pages, on which multiple lines are underscored. Under the title, in blue pen: Juan Manuel García-Junco, April 1986. My father was around twenty-four at the time, the same age Yourcenar was when she wrote the book, according to the prologue of the 1970s edition in my hand. It's Alfaguara's old design, simpler and neater than the one they use today, without images or gloss. Requisite smell of cigarettes, check; yellowed pages, check.

Judging by the underlining, the book made quite an impression on a young Juan Manuel who was not yet so very H. Pascal. When I read the maxims that twenty-four-year-old Marguerite puts in Alexis's mouth, I often marvel at her tiny observational treasures. Other times, as is only natural, I find them simplistic. She herself enters into dialogue with her character (the past version of herself) twenty years after writing the book and says that she declined the chance to update it because all the statements that seemed anachronistic in the present were part of how the character was constructed. Alexis was Alexis, and that was it. He was going to die just like he was born. Alexis shows us the danger of not changing, of getting stranded in time—especially for those of us who don't have the luxury of being made purely of letters.

Above all, this book is a love letter to Monique, the wife Alexis leaves in order to be true to his sexual orientation and to himself. It's also the account of a life that isn't near its end, but rather the end of the lie that has kept it safe. Alexis tries to find an explanation for his homosexuality in his upbringing among women, and this is one of the lines of thinking Yourcenar rejects years later. The character, however, insists, rooting around in his past to find reasons for his present. It is one of those books that searches for the meaning of life and urges its readers to do the same. Unfortunately, the path of paternal archaeology has led me to look for keys to a life that isn't mine. I might be missing out on an excellent therapeutic exercise.

I think about the death of my grandfather Juan Manuel, about the three boys and the little girl who were left without a father or any money. I think about a phrase voiced by Alexis: "The past, no matter how little one thinks about it, is infinitely more stable than the present, and as such seems to be of much greater consequence." If this book has been anything, it has been the search for the keys to the unravelling of a life. I realise now, as I read *Alexis*, that I've been looking for them as if they were a single entity and not, after all, an accounting of moments and decisions, of a leopard and his spots. And also, naturally, of context and other pressures.

Even so, I refuse to give up my search for the missing key. I feel like I'm scratching my way towards something bigger.

*

I open the box of papers I took from his house—a part, in some twisted way, of his library. Many of the things he saved in here date back to his reading of *Alexis*. In my search for memories that help me trace a chronological line leading to disaster, I look through a stack of Italian-style brown paper notebooks, the kind they ask you to bring to kindergarten for drawing in. In them, my father had made a scrapbook of his first pieces to appear in the newspaper, back in the early eighties. Strangely, he signed them as Juan Manuel Payán—an homage, I guess, to his chemist grandfather. Interviews with famous writers, coverage of cultural events, pages and pages of normal, well-written texts. In line with all this, his credentials: one from Radio Cadena Nacional in 1988 that identifies him as an international reporter, and another, dated 1991, from Novedades Editores that has him as a staff writer. I guess this is the period that editor I met at one of those parties where all the intrigue of the publishing world converged was talking about. He said that my father wrote the only review his first book ever received and even invited him onto his radio pro-gramme. Those were the days of wool blazers with patches on the elbows, the whole look of a checked shirt tucked into jeans and his first thick-framed glasses. Of the well-groomed Mr. Writer who dedicates his novels to his wife, *la elfa*.

I begin to fit these pieces together with what I already know, and the unravelling of my father's life makes more sense. My mother didn't only give me a notebook of realities project-ing dreams, she also gave me a grey folder. Inside, those three letters that signal all modern intrigue: USB. And even more so: external hard drive. The storage on our electronic devices is like the darkest depths of our souls. The highest highs and the lowest lows, all there in your search history. Licit and illicit passions, morbid fascinations, assorted joys, hobbies, loves, obsessions, rabbit holes. Secrets.

In brief: everything you hope no one, maybe not even yourself, ever sees all together.

I click, I read, I see; my body reacts by contracting in places that shouldn't contract—like, for example, at the sides of my head, from which veins now visibly throb. To say nothing of my calves, which, in an all-out war against lightness, are two rocks on the verge of cramping. Even so, I don't get up. I just keep clicking and clicking.

With all the private information that passes before my eyes, I probably should tear them out like Oedipus did. I continue, though I know I'll regret it. What is seen can't be unseen.

*

Two days later, I want to throw everything in the trash, stop my research. I want to blurt out heinous things that I feel horrible about even thinking, even if no one ever knows. My chest throbs, it catches the opening lines of Tatiana Țîbuleac's *The Summer My Mother Had Green Eyes* the way someone might catch a scent: "The morning I hated her more than ever before, my mother turned thirty-nine. She was short and fat, stupid and ugly. She was the most useless mother who ever lived."

*

Wily, Alexis whispers: "Confidences, my dear, are always insidious when not aimed at simplifying the other's life."

Twenty-four-year-old Juan Manuel's underlining could very well speak with his ghost.

154

*

In April of 2019, the musician and writer Armando Vega-Gil was called out in the #MeToo movement for having abused a minor several years earlier. He took his life the next day, leaving behind a confusing, ominous letter and lots of questions. My father was about as sad as I'd ever seen him. And he wasn't alone. Several men of that generation, friends of his I'd had some contact with, went into a state of mourning they weren't equipped to process. Between unconvincing diatribes about the "presumption of innocence," my father wrote to my mother, my brother and me in our group chat about how painful it was for him that someone would feel so backed into a corner by these accusations that he would feel the need to leave this world. I find his stupor reasonable and sincere: decades of complicity, the fondness you feel towards someone—those things don't just evaporate. The accusations become a sword unsheathed to blame someone else for a decision as personal as suicide. While we fought by text message, I couldn't stop thinking how, though his pain was legitimate, disqualifying the accusation wasn't the only way of confronting his loss. Lydia Cacho, another friend of Vega-Gil, gave a radio interview in a very different tone—one that allowed space for her pain but didn't discredit the accusations or excuse the deceased for the choices he'd made. Still, it was clear that my father's arguments were also coming from his own experience, from a place that remained unnamed.

If so many men close to my father were so distressed without even being close to Vega-Gil, it's because this was about something much bigger. The case held a mirror up to many men in the intellectual circles of that generation (and the following ones). The shocking tolerance for how young women, sometimes minors, become prey in plain view is and will be the source of many stories with similar endings: a woman feeling violated, a man incapable of recognising his own wrongdoing. Unless masculinity changes and adequate conditions for the repair of damages are created.

Between the fascination with the idea of The Artist, cults of personality and the fixation some men have with presenting themselves as the teachers and sponsors of women half- or one-third as old as them, bohemian[24] environments turn out to be particularly thorny for fresh-faced young women stepping into a new world without much judgement or guidance, and sometimes without patience. I'm sure an imbalanced relationship like that (teacher/celebrity and student/ingenue) offers something to the younger party, but the violence inherent to that obvious hierarchy—because there's no hiding who's in charge—could do her harm that lasts the rest of her life. Some manage to turn the tables and turn the episode into a long goodbye, but many others find themselves needing to live with the consequences.

That joke about Leonardo DiCaprio—how he went down with the Titanic and when he came back up, he'd forgotten how to date women over twenty-five—applies to writers just like it does to actors. Not all cases, of course, are the same. Some relationships that involve an unequal power dynamic due to age, fame or money aren't violent; the two parties strike a balance, and the more privileged of them finds a way to be decent. A relationship with a man twenty years older than you can be fertile ground for discovering things as a couple,

---

24 BOHEMIAN: A woman might hold the belief that certain words should never be used, words that sound like bad music and stale alcohol—and yet, that fateful hour has come.

hopping on the seesaw of privilege (because there are other ways of experiencing privilege, ways that have nothing to do with age and gender), and learning how to work towards something from new vantage points. But that's not usually the case. If the shoe fits.

*

I'm sure that the blow of #MeToo and Vega-Gil's death struck my father most deeply as reflections of the end of an era. Of his era. His mind and emotions were having a hard time adjusting to this kind of change. After all, when he was growing up many of the behaviours denounced by #MeToo were condoned or even commended. I guess the Vega-Gil accusation will hit harder if you yourself have been tempted by similar sins, even if the details were different. A time bomb begins its sinister ticking, and you become painfully aware of a moral shift in an era increasingly unwilling to quietly accept what others had suffered in silence.

All those Alexises stranded in time like a book written in the thirties.

*

Seeing my father constantly surrounded by women much younger than him, watching him cling to the idea of being their teacher in all senses of the word, was more than a little hard for me. A man in search of a cult following. Abusing the imagery of fantastic literature, Alfonso says he was searching for The Great Elf. I translate it as the same mix of machismo and racism we grow up being spoon-fed, which hordes still carry with them to their graves.

Maybe that's why our relationship grew so tense over the years. The less tolerance I had for what he wanted, the less we could stand one another. I was his antagonist; I saw him as neither a teacher nor an idol. At one point during the numb moments surrounding my parents' divorce, I overheard him on the phone with a woman. He was upset because she had gone to an event with him and another man, and everyone there had noticed. That was how I learned he had something resembling a girlfriend.

A couple of months later, when we were no longer living under the same roof, he introduced me to the girl in passing. The first thing that wrung my insides was that she couldn't have been more than twenty-five; the second was her hostility towards me. She clearly had no interest in getting to know me. My father was over forty. I was sixteen. I never heard anything else about her, but Alfonso told me she was just using my father as a budget sugar daddy, that she actually had a boyfriend her own age and often brought him to events and passed him the beers my father bought her. That my father made my uncle sign off on her servicio social and she never even so much as thanked him. That she broke my father's heart and Goliardos went to hell because he couldn't handle it. I don't know what the real story was. All I have is that moment in El Circo Volador, which was uncomfortable for her and me both. All I have is the physical memory of unease. After that, there was no turning back. He went from my mother, who was a few years older than him, to suddenly aiming twenty years younger. As is the case with so many men, he kept aging, but his taste never did. Who would have thought that my father and Leo would have something in common.

In any case, he never introduced me like that to anyone

ever again. No other woman was as important to him for the next twenty years.

*

The loss of his friends, who were dying off one by one. The deafening end of Vega-Gil. The waters of time washing away many of his foundational assumptions. The possibility that what little he had might be ripped from him. The lack of future, the surplus of past.

*

What he didn't entirely grasp then—though I think he did, a bit later—is that his blind spot was much bigger than he could admit. And that it contained the violence experienced by women close to him.

My grandmother's house is tiny. When I was a little girl, every time the family got together there, furniture and people needed to be moved around in order to get from one place to another. My cousins, my brother and I were all growing, while in an unnatural and unverifiable turn of events my grand-mother's home was shrinking. Always neat, always pretty and unexpectedly modern, it was the exact opposite of how the cliché would have you imagine the home of a woman in her seventies (now her nineties). As if in solidarity with her apart-ment in Cuautitlán Izcalli, years ago she, too, began to shrink. My cyborg grandmother carries in her body a tempestuous record of falls, from the one that gave her a titanium elbow to the one after which she ended up with silicone between two of the vertebrae in her neck.

One Sunday not so many years ago, my father, my brother

and I were what didn't fit in her microspace. I don't know how it all happened. These eruptions, the kind that start with something trivial like a football match and end with someone getting a black eye, are rarely predictable. We were immersed in the usual, a conversation grounded entirely in love and the desire to be there with each other, a conversation that goes beyond canned phrases, beyond "how have you been" and "when I die," and someone lit the fuse. I don't remember whether it was my father or my brother, but they were in full agreement: reggaeton is degrading and you can't be a feminist if you dance to it. Or maybe it was more personal: How could I? I replied like I always did back when I still bothered with provocations: Do you challenge your friends when they say sexist crap the way you just challenged me and my preferences? The question is, of course, rhetorical, though there may be brave souls out there who would venture a reply. I don't know if someone did that day, because the next thing I remember is me yelling that taxi drivers used to masturbate outside my high school. I'm sure there was something that connected those two moments in the conversation, and I'm sure that something was expressed in high decibels. But by the time the masturbating taxi drivers appeared on the scene, everything had shifted to an attempt to calm me down. Unfortunately, by that point there was no calming me, and to make matters worse, I was in Cuautitlán Izcalli (which is to say, far) without many options for escape. My aunt shut herself in my grandmother's room with me and said they'd never understand. Then my grandmother's hairdresser—who'd made a house call because the bionic granny was wearing a shiny new neck brace and couldn't move—joined in. "They'll never understand, they don't live it."

When I emerged from the room, my father hugged me. Stiff and teary, I didn't hug him back. He asked me if anyone had ever raped me. It was hard to miss the fear in his voice. It was also hard to miss his lack of sensitivity in just tossing the question out there. Sometimes you have to focus on the intention, rather than the act itself. The intention here was loving.

He was a caring man, and I was a cold woman.

Something in him changed after that. In the time he had left, he was a little more empathetic.

*

Alexis says: "Perhaps we have not paid enough attention to the fact that the problem of sensual freedom, in all its forms, is largely a problem of freedom of expression. It seems that, from generation to generation, the propensities and acts vary little; what does change, in contrast, is how far the zone of silence extends around them and how thick the layers of lies."

*

I peel away the layers of lies and the zones of silence. Today I tell myself: be careful when digging around in the closet for skeletons. The success of Goliardos in my late teens was its swan song; the original collective was about to disband. I don't really know how it all happened, but my father's fight with Alfonso was a mortal blow and I was a little bit to blame for it, though I only discovered this today, thanks (but no thanks) to this investigation.

Alfonso was, as was so often the case, the origin of the revelation and a social network, the medium itself.

A message appears: he is writing to say that he's wanted to ask me something for a long time, to check something that never added up, but that it's "delicate." "Fire away," I said, feeling bulletproof after months of rooting through my father's library and the memories it released.

"Sixteen or eighteen years ago, maybe, did you get caught taking clothes from a store without paying for them?" I love that he went to the trouble of using the euphemism "taking without paying" rather than just saying clear out what it was: stealing.

I tell him that I did, and he replies that "a weird thing happened at Goliardos that never quite sat right. What came next was confusing and sad."

*

It's hard to understand how much suffering we cause our parents; how much they stop being and doing because of their progeny. In *Anna Karenina*, Darya Alexandrovna, a noblewoman in her thirties, travels to the countryside with her six little scions. After a few practical issues at the outset, she manages to feel comfortable, if not peaceful—an impossibility with all those kids running around. But: "these cares and anxieties were for Darya Alexandrovna the sole happiness possible [...] And besides, hard though it was for the mother to bear the dread of illness, the illnesses themselves, and the grief of seeing signs of evil propensities in her children—the children themselves were even now repaying her in small joys for her sufferings. Those joys were so small that they passed unnoticed, like gold in sand, and at bad moments she could see nothing but the pain, nothing but sand; but there were good moments too when she saw nothing but the joy, nothing but gold."

What does it mean for someone to bring you into the world? As a daughter who is only a daughter, I try to see beyond this side of giving and receiving life. I look at the children around me, the way they demand and cry, kick and smash. Small tyrannies that don't end with adulthood. What does change is the flip side: as much as small children demand, they give back in love. A love so sincere it annihilates everything around it. Then people get older, and that sincerity is lost. I'm not saying there's no way to return love after childhood, but I am saying that demands and reproaches cut deeper when they come from an adult and that manifestations of love change over time. Children don't cause pain because they want to. They learn little by little from the selfishness necessary to build their self-confidence. Adults are another story. The day comes when our parents have to forgive us, even if we keep repeating that eternal line about how they put us on this planet. Some people never stop making excuses for themselves based on wounds inflicted on them when very young, and though it's true that childhood trauma never goes away, part of growing up is taking responsibility for the places you're broken.

*

My father, however, wasn't one of those people who toss everything that goes wrong back at the past. No, he was more old school, the kind who would sweep everything under the rug of non-introspection. Why blame the past when you can blame other people? Let's not forget that The Great Loser fights against an unjust world. The male Great Loser also fights against the senseless moralising that seeks to change things he doesn't believe need changing. His heart may be in the right place, as I'm sure my father's was, but his blind spot is a hurdle.

Though the process of his really getting stuck there was a slow one, I think I witnessed the seed of what was to come on one of those canned weekend visits permitted and ordered by

163

custodial arrangement (accursed term). My brother, his eyes shining with puberty, and me, with the rage typical of adolescence. My father, reclining on the couch with one leg crossed over the other in the shape of a four, as he tended to do, in a brown wool vest over a black Goliardos shirt. (The one I hold close sometimes?) Behind the scenes, a daughter, angry and closed off from the world, cutting herself in Technical Drawing class; a boy shouting and cursing, totally impossible. And, of course, a mother dealing with the aftermath of the shipwreck from Monday through Saturday. Swimming, perhaps, in the guilt of our pain as well as her own.

Back to the room: on stage, a father with one leg crossed over the other telling a son, "Don't listen to your mother, she's crazy." And me, thinking that he doesn't spend any real time with my brother, he just shows up and acts cool and does nothing but talk her down, whereas she never, ever says a negative word about him, not even when she clearly wants to. I wish I could have said these things to him in the moment, just like I wish I could have said something when he complained about how much of his salary he had to pay my mother, as if he weren't talking to one of the people on the receiving end of that money. Maybe he would have moved out of that place where he was getting stuck, even if only a little.

Alfonso always says that my father was an alpha male, and all I think of when I hear those words are the worst things a man can be.

*

In order to process (or hide from) what Alfonso told me in his message, I think about the fourth step in Alcoholics Anonymous, the one that invites you to make a searching and fearless moral inventory of your life. In addition to listing where our instincts went awry in order to take responsibility for our actions and their consequences for other people, this step also asks what function pain and resentment have in your life. When this question was first presented to me, the idea that resentment could be useful seemed ridiculous to me. After months of thinking about my father in a thousand different ways, I realise that yes, at least in my case, resentment has allowed me to maintain an image, a tension that has outlived even death itself. It has also allowed me to justify my actions and attitudes and absolve myself of guilt—or else sweep it under the rug. I, too, have a way with a broom.

Our communities—our family and all that surrounds it or, better still, whatever constellation we choose to call family—are composed of intricate round-trip connections. The wounds we inflict on one another are two-way streets with many ways in and out. We all live in the teeming petri dish that is a shared history. I wonder how much my coldness contributed to my father's pain and to what extent, in my questioning the validity of his choices, did I make him feel like more of a failure? (*Did* he feel like a failure, or is that my fear talking?) I think about how many excuses I've made for myself based on things he did. I confront the magnitude of actions and reactions. As often happens, he and I found ourselves in a stalemate we couldn't break for years. We dug in our heels, in the deepest sense of the term.

*

If the story Alfonso told me doesn't illustrate that one mistake leads to another, I don't know what would. One book fair after another during some spring in Mexico City, a festival in the Zócalo and finally a new idea: Goliardos would get a new (minimalist!) look. White cover, cleaner typeface, ISBN, distribution in bookstores. The wet dream of my love for bourgeois aesthetics. Goliardos would be domesticated, enter the mainstream. This was—surprise, surprise—partly my father's idea. It was time to emerge from underground. He and Alfonso designed the new image together and got ready to get to work. They had fifty thousand pesos to complete their mission. More than enough.

Alfonso says: "We had three events that went incredibly well, and then one day he says to me, 'This thing happened and I had to use all the money for bail.'"

"This thing," meaning: me, leaving El Palacio de Hierro with seven thousand pesos worth of stolen clothing on me. "This thing," meaning: the most agonising night of my life, the source of all my nightmares in the coming years. The emergency.

"I had to use all the money to get her out of jail," said Pascal to Alfonso. Goliardos was left without a cent. Not one. Alfonso suspected he was lying because that was the period when my father was most hung up on the aforementioned girl and he saw her going around showing off all sorts of things, books, a new computer.

"That was when I said, 'You know what, arsehole? I don't buy it.' I was furious, and to top it off, he tried to tell me, 'But look, there's five hundred left over for you.'"

It's sad that Alfonso didn't believe him, and that his doubt ended up destroying the delicate thread that just barely held them together at the time. Sad but understandable, because my father had always had a questionable relationship with money. Like the benevolent tyrant he was, you had no choice but to trust that his administrative skills and his intentions were good.

"I'm sure he used some of the money to get you out of jail, but not all of it."

It's true. The sum required to keep me out of juvie, as far as I know, didn't match the total. My father spent the rest of the money, however much or little there was, on something else. On what? And, much more importantly: Why?

*

Instead of trying and potentially failing: self-sabotage. Let's dynamite the foundations of our new home before any future leaks have a chance to damage the walls. Let's burn the ships before we reach port to avoid the risk of a crushing defeat. Let's be Spartacus, but let's give up right when we get our hands on the weapons that might lead us to victory.

*

Alexis says: "At first, I thought it was a question of avoiding all occasions for sin; I soon realized that our actions are but symptoms: it is our nature that must change."

*

In my mind, a mosaic of recollections that confirm the hypothesis stemming from the grey folder and Alfonso's story. A) One day, when my father was already in his late fifties, I brought my partner to a meal with him. He wasn't sick yet, but he didn't have his own place. Instead, he'd been renting a room from some lady "until he found something else." He told us, over a subpar steak, that he needed to find an apartment soon because he couldn't write if he didn't fuck. I felt like saying thank you, I absolutely did not need to know that. B) When my father started to go missing from work for long periods of time, my uncle called me one day to say that he'd tried to kill himself once when he was younger, as though that were proof that he was on the verge of doing it again. That phrase became a morbid echo I still hear to this day. A friend of my father's, a bookseller and distributor known as The Dwarf, found himself flush with money and decided to start a publishing house. He got the idea that my father could run it and commissioned four books for the catalogue. A few months later, my father presented the fruits of his labour. "Pascal walks in and hands him... four Goliardos chapbooks," says Alfonso.

The Dwarf was, unsurprisingly, not pleased. Pascal had the opportunity to make it happen and the backing of someone who believed in him and in Goliardos. And he didn't do it. D) Alfonso tells me that, during one of my father's many periods of dire financial straits, he offered him a monthly column in *Gourmet* magazine, where he was an editor. At the same time, another of his students, Arturo J. Flores, offered to publish his work in *Playboy*. My father told Alfonso that the assignment sounded like a drag and handed Arturo one of the printouts he gave away at El Chopo of "Father and Son," a story that had already been published all over, telling Arturo to transcribe it. And so, just like that, he rejected both jobs—one explicitly, and the other, tacitly. As time went by, he clung more fervently to the discourse that the world was, generally speaking, full of cretins.

*

Alexis, again insightfully: "It is hard not to believe oneself superior when one is suffering."

*

I thought that researching my father's life would bring me some kind of redemption, but these days it seems that the more I learn, the angrier I get—with myself, and with him. I can't help but think of axiomatic, categorical phrases that sound so awful in my head I can't imagine putting them on paper. That fourth step isn't going so well.

I think that when I started to write, deep down I wanted to do justice to our relationship, but above all to him. I wanted to celebrate his life story and his legacy from a place of tenderness and reconciliation. Héctor Abad Faciolince's *Oblivion* comes back to mind, particularly how the author manages to make his readers love his father, even if only a little. The effect must be easier to achieve when your father is an activist on the right side of history whose imperfections, at least the ones Abad presents to us in a closed casket, fade far into the background relative to the man's greatness.

What am I supposed to do with mine, who put so much energy into self-sabotage? What am I supposed to do with the guilt our relationship generates in me to this day? What good does it do me? Alexis offers no advice on this matter.

*

"Life is a desire, not a meaning." And if the desire isn't fulfilled, does one stop desiring? Without desire, there is no meaning.

*

Then suddenly, interference: a conversation with my brother
that reminds me that things are never as simple as we think,
and that people are more complex than the idea we have of
them. Among the incomprehensible swarm of objects on my
bookshelves in my father's apartment, a collection of monster
figurines that had come with our McDonald's Happy Meals.
Some of the loveliest moments of my childhood happened
in the presence of one of those plastic, probably radioactive,
hamburgers. Even now when I think of those burgers, I feel
something like a flash of happiness.[25]

One of the first things I did when we arrived to clean out
my father's house was to remove all the decorations and knick-
knacks from the plastic crates he'd been using as bookshelves.
The figurines went into the bag of probable trash, since I'd
been wondering for years why my father had saved that Count
Dracula with his grimy coffin and that shiny plastic Loch Ness
Monster. Hours later, my brother commandeered my discrimi-
nating selection of rubbish and took the monsters. He told me
that he'd been alone with my father one day not long before,
and when my father noticed those Happy Meal spawn he had
said that the part of his divorce from my mother that had hurt
him the most was not getting to see us anymore. And then, the
miracle: he burst out in tears. I imagine my brother did, too.
How crazy, and at the same time how logical that the proximity of death should have put him in touch with his feelings
like that. He never cried with me. Still, that was all I needed to
cling to this story. Not everything is a bid for control, mistakes

---

25 HAPPINESS: Who would have thought that the flash of this rare good isn't
gold or silver, but instead of a delicate transparency that vanishes into the air?

and losses; there is also love and care. He took good care of us, and he loved us even more.

*

I stand. I breathe deep. I search the shelves for another book that might serve me as a guide, but the magic of random selection is blocked by emotion. In all the tumult, I sit on the cold floor and use a bookshelf as an uncomfortable backrest. My cat sits on my legs. I look her in the eyes and ask: what is this book for? She looks at me with either understanding or indifference. I resign myself to that and ask another question, this one more complex: what is the limit when we write about someone else's life? Would it bother you, kitty dearest, to appear in a book?

The other person (or cat) cannot, by definition, respond within the text. Though it can be cited in long paragraphs, emails, messages, lines that counterbalance the story's orientation, the fact remains that the text is impervious to external replies. There are other mechanisms. I think about Vanessa Springora, the French journalist who, with a single powerful statement, laid waste to the narrative of Gabriel Matzneff, the writer who seduced her when she was thirteen and he was fifty. Matzneff published numerous volumes describing the relationship he had with the minor according to his personal and irrefutable criteria, and then one day Springora's book comes along to expose him and his sustained paedophilic manipulations. Two ways of talking about someone else's life.

I also think about perhaps the most famous writer of non-fiction novels, Emmanuel Carrère and his ongoing dispute with his ex-wife Hélène Devynck; I think about the contract that prohibits him from mentioning her or their son in his work, which left a distinct hole in the middle of his novel

Yoga but not did not save him from a lawsuit for not having fully observed the restrictions she imposed. The author claims to have written only what was absolutely necessary to portray his own grief over the divorce. Hélène did not agree.

I wonder about all those books from days gone by that described, perverted and disturbed the lives of others; I wonder about those secondary and principal characters flattened between the pages by other quills. I wonder how many protagonists and secondary characters read themselves and cursed, how many of them faced trouble in their daily lives because of an artistic choice, and it seems to me that in this era of autofiction and tell-all social media, a line is tensing as never before.

The fantasy that we're writing about our own lives is shaken to its foundations when we see ourselves through other eyes, and a harsh judgement takes new weight when it becomes the printed word. I don't think anyone will ever solve the problem of what we are allowed to borrow—unless the art dies altogether.

In this book, I'm talking about a dead man I loved. His ashes run through my veins in the form of shared genetic material and so much of who I am. We're so close that in my worst nightmares I watch each punch I swing at him bring another of equal force right back at me. I don't want to hurt the ones I love. I don't want to hurt anyone, not even the ones I hate. Sometimes I think I don't have the guts to write this book and picture the convenience of a more distant fiction. Novelising, erasing guilty parties, twisting history; sacrificing in the name of aesthetics, but also in the name of decorum.

I return to *Oblivion* and am faced with the tenderness of Héctor Abad Faciolince and a story that doesn't hurt his father but instead leaves a sweet taste in the mouth when the author speaks from the place of profound love he declares in the book's opening lines. "The boy, me, loved the man, his father, above all things. He loved him more than God. One day I had to choose between God and my dad, and I chose my dad." Even in the darkest moments, even in his defects and his excesses, we feel an embrace that holds his father safe.

Then I search for a counterpoint. In *Draw a Heavy Curtain*, another book about a writer who is a daughter writing about her writer father. Pilar Donoso uses the diaries of her father, José Donoso—which he himself donated to a university—in order to reconstruct an inner world previously unknown to her. José Donoso, a giant of the Boom,[26] reveals himself to her as a man with serious mental health issues who went so far as to think that she wanted to kill him, who theorised about the many ways Pilarcita—what he called her in order to distinguish her from his wife—intended to destroy him. In the pages of his diaries, for example, the man refers to Pilar (not Pilarcita) as a fat cow who leaves her teeth lying around the house and wonders how she could expect him to fuck her. Staring at all this straight on, Pilar Donoso patiently weaves the biography she promised her father she would write, and for which she even conducted a series of interviews.

I read and re-read and recognise so many things… I laugh, I cry, I get angry, I forgive, I cry again; I feel disappointed, I put him on a pedestal, and I forgive him again because I loved him immensely.

Like me, Pilar plunged into the depths of a black sea, where no light reaches. She never stopped reading, even though her rage and her shame probably demanded it. I feel

---

26 BOOM: The cartoon sound of a bomb exploding; the sound, I suppose, of a group of dudes who wrote a few great books and then made (continue to make) some pretty appalling statements.

close to her when I dig around the hidden corners of a mind I'll never know. She asserts that you "should never know the most intimate thoughts of anyone, least of all your parents," and while I fundamentally agree with her, I still envy her for that access to the inaccessible. Those letters, those diaries, that reality that was her father's unbalanced mind.

Draw a Heavy Curtain begins with an idea for a story as described by José Donoso in a letter: a writer's daughter gets her hands on her father's diaries, which have been left to a university, and—after writing a book based on them—she kills herself. Pilar Donoso died by suicide one year after publishing the book about her and her father. I imagine that this decision had to do with the book's reception and the knowledge that she exposed her father, but also and above all, with what she uncovered. There are things that are best left unseen, unknown. But, as we all know, once they've been seen, they can never be unseen.[27] This includes, of course, our own role in the stories we tell. Our responsibility.

It's hard to draw the line between what you want to know and the abyss that opens at your feet when you begin a search that could lead to sinister encounters. Especially the encounter with yourself. Quite a few myths have been written about that.

*

Alexis says: "I did not know that disgust is one of obsession's many forms, and that if we desire something it is easier to think of it with horror than not to think of it." And I wonder what remained in the sixty-year-old of the twenty-four-year-old

---

27   TO UNSEE: Racing in vain to draw that curtain right back to where it probably should have stayed in the first place.

Juan Manuel who read and listened to Alexis. Whether he, like Yourcenar's character, managed to break down the walls he had built around himself. Whether his rejection of the mainstream was him coming out of the closet of intellectual elite pretension, or whether it was just another of The Great Loser's gambits. I guess those aren't mutually exclusive.

SEVENTH: THE SCRAWL WE ARE

La ridícula idea de no volver a verte, Rosa Montero, Seix Barral, 2013. Net contents: a moving glimpse into the life and diaries of Marie Curie (and the death of her love).

"From the ruins, you obsess about the moment just before the quake, turning it over and over in your mind. If only I had known! you say. But no, you didn't know."

The title drew me in like a magnet. I arrived at this book selfishly: I wanted a break and, immersed as I was in morbidity, its lightness and liveliness seemed like a breath of fresh air. Strange that a book about death should have that effect. I'm not convinced it was my father, but someone read to page 130, where the jacket flap is inserted. (My material analysis reveals that the first pages, the ones inside the flap, are darker than the others; the poor book must have undergone a process like tanning, but the opposite: sun-bleaching.) I say "someone" because there are a few pink post-its stuck here and there, a highly unusual detail. The delicate pencil underlining looks like it was done with a ruler, and the writing in the margins is miniscule, whereas his was always expansive, unafraid to take up space on the page—just like he was in life. I also picture him, without any evidence beyond having known him for thirty years, getting stopped in his tracks by the title, the same one that made me pull the book from the shelf. I'm certain: what I find brilliant, he would have found corny.

In summary, the book seems to have been given as a gift or accidentally left behind. A secret affair? An attempt to make him read something he'd never buy on his own? A failure on the part of one of the women in his life? I don't want to know.

The Ridiculous Idea of Never Seeing You Again is many things at once, including the story of two women in mourning.

Rosa Montero writes about the moment when Marie Curie is widowed after her husband Pierre is mowed down by a car, in order to talk about the loss of her own husband to cancer. Two deaths: the same and yet so different. Talking about the life of another (or the lives of many others) in order to talk about one's own.

*

The need to talk about the people we lose in universal terms comes from the very logical drive to feel ourselves accompanied in our loss. With pain of that magnitude, hugs from our loved ones will never be enough to fill the void and bring meaning back to our lives. And yet that's exactly what we need to make happen, because that black hole is trying to occupy the centre of our existence, and even though it won't ever go away, how awful would it be if it remained the thing that rules us.

Reading a book about death is part of a healing ritual, regardless of whether that reading happens before or after the event, because a fundamental characteristic of rituals is that they are a space of shared emotions. I join this long procession of mourners who read one another, like a self-help group that transcends space and time.

My name is Aura and I've lost someone.

*

Marie Curie also kept a diary, but in second person and much more structured than the meandering investigation I've been working on these past seven months. One might say it was a letter containing all the things she never managed to say to

178

Pierre. Writing the ending she never got to have the way she would have wanted it, as Rosa Montero says. I doubt anyone ever feels that all accounts were properly settled when it comes to the death of a loved one. There's always a need to write the ending that was never resolved, and that writing (whether it's done on paper or only with thoughts) is, precisely, part of the mourning process. It occurred to me that it might be therapeutic to do just that: relive the last hours we shared.

Except there weren't any. Or there were, but in such a contemporary sense that it's sad. Our last interaction was him sending me a text message with a link to "The Origins of Popular Literature and Poetry" by Antonio Gramsci, one day before he died. I replied "cool," and he sent me a little blue thumbs-up. As simple as that. Our final exchange ended with an emoticon. Could be worse, I think, despite the fact I never read the essay.

*

The Ridiculous Idea of Never Seeing You Again proposes a few interesting exercises. For example, Rosa Montero writes: "All these little things, in effect, make up a person. They are our basic formula, the unique scrawl of our lives." I come up with a preliminary list of little details, like "No one else will ever make a fake German sausage soup like my father, for the simple reason that he always invented the recipe on the spot." Or "No one else will ever use radioactive green reusable shopping bags to store dozens of books to give away as gifts," and "No one else will ever walk at that ridiculous speed through a packed metro station with those damned shopping bags on his shoulder while his daughter runs behind him, unable to catch up because of all the people around and her much shorter legs."

Then there's: "No one else will ever say the same phrase each time he's in a taxi driving through the housing project where we used to live: *careful, please, it's a two-way street*, always with the same intonation" and "No one else will ever throw such wild tantrums, like that classic moment when he woke up angry one Saturday morning because my brother and I were bickering and ripped the VHS that was the cause of our discord out of the machine, leaving it unusable."

As I do this exercise, even his worst moments seem endearing. I'm surprised. Is this the process of sanctification that tends to occur automatically when someone dies? Wanting to avoid that temptation, I try to remember more things about him but quickly realise I can't. I guess these are the memories that pop up in daily life when you least need them. Either that, or I'm forgetting his essential lines and soon he'll live on only as a rough sketch. Maybe it's not a bad idea to start thinking about the individual scrawl of the people around us before they're gone. To write them in the present tense.

*

The book answers:

... It makes sense that we should battle against forgetting, because it is the final defeat before our great enemy, death, repulsive destroyer of sweetness, divider of multitudes, decimator of palaces and builder of tombs, as it is called in the *Thousand and One Nights*, a book well acquainted with humankind's unequal combat against the Reaper.

It's a shame I have such a bad memory, but thank goodness for books and their perfect recall. This way, I can stick everything I want to get back in here and assiduously release the rest to the waters of time. Perhaps ease is to be found in this balance. The logic being that if everything is written down, I can free my mind from the obligation of being a museum.

*

Despite the temptation to turn my father into a saint, I haven't managed to rebuild what I lost, in part because I lost it long before his death. The resentment I've carried for years tastes like a broken dream, like losing a hero and finding a man.

It's normal for children to view their parents as heroes. They are, after all, the ones who save them from death on a daily basis; in the case of fathers, they also have a lot of good press on their side. The problem is that we realise at some point that our parents are fallible and then, instead of recognising them as human, we get angry about their shortcomings. This reconciliation with their singularity, with their existence as people separate from us, is slow and painful—to varying degrees, maybe, but it always is. And that whole encounter with reality is surrounded by a narrative we tell ourselves.

Memory is an invention, a story we rewrite every day (what I remember today of my childhood is not the same as what I remembered twenty years ago), which means that our identities are also fictional because they're based on memory.

I'm an expert in stories. We all are. The problem is that sometimes those life stories stagnate and turn into a tree fallen across a highway instead of a way of gaining perspective.

How did my father narrate himself to himself? According to Rosa Montero, "...it's a question of narration. Of the story we tell about ourselves to ourselves. Learning to live is a process of the #word." My father and the way he saw himself through the lens of *us versus them* is an example of a narrative that, while somewhat based on real events, was also rooted in

181

the rest of his personal history. I imagine that the rupture he experienced as a child catalysed his need to create a family that wouldn't leave him, a merry-go-round with him at its centre. His students were that family.

I've just become what I swore to destroy: the psychoanalyst of one of my characters.

I'm tempted to mention how paradoxical it is that someone who dedicated his entire life to words couldn't construct a gratifying personal narrative for himself, but to frame it like that is to overlook many things. First, because we never know ourselves as well as we might like. Second, because even though he studied psychology, it's hard to say how capable he was of self-scrutiny, given that he was a man with a traumatic childhood raised to ignore his feelings. He came from a long line of highly intelligent but neurotic and excessively rational men.[28]

How much did the idea of success weigh on him, in a family with so many successes? And the idea of failure? I know from experience: the mere thought of failing is enough to destroy you; if I'm wrong, give me back all those nights back I spent captive to pessimistic hallucinations and teary self-flagellation, feeling like a failure in nearly all aspects of life. Now I see that seed in me, and it is also my inheritance. It's not that I blame him entirely, but much of what I know about the literary world came from my desire not to be him, not to see things the way he did.

These words sound so harsh. Now I'm beginning to read it differently. Now I'm even managing, sometimes, to think of him again as an ephemeral hero.

---

28   RATIONAL: Death to reason without a body through which to circulate as blood. It is, at the end of the day, another form of madness.

*

An interesting fact from the book: according to a respected study, people whose spouses have died are happier than people who have gotten divorced. It turns out to be easier to forgive someone who has died than someone who has caused us pain—in the end, they can't hurt us anymore, at least not directly. Death, generally speaking, isn't evidence that something went wrong: it's a tragedy. I suspect that this also has something to do with narratives and the creation of heroes and saints.

I'm suddenly invaded by a thought so obvious it's almost banal: my father was heartbroken after the divorce, too. The suffering wasn't limited to the house where my mother, my brother and I remained—he had to create a new home, as angry and forlorn as he was. I imagine that first night in his miniscule new apartment, the first of many; he is lit by the dim glow of a table lamp, staring at his lonely bookshelves. I imagine an initial moment of euphoria ("all this is mine, this is my kingdom"), followed by a silence as impossible to control as these images crowding my mind, a silence that takes over everything despite the Yes album playing on full blast. The emptiness, the sound of something twisting in the pit of your stomach. The awareness that you won't be living with the woman you were married to for more than a decade, and for whom you now think you hold more hatred than love. The pain of your mistakes and the mistakes of others. Your angry daughter, your tearful son. Under another roof.

Now that I have the compassion I lacked then, I can see we were all in the same unsteady boat, even if we didn't know it. Pain locks you inside yourself; time offers perspective.

*

I try to embrace the bittersweet taste this idea leaves in my mouth. To be generous. And it's from that place that I try to tell myself the story of his attempts at relationships after the divorce. Of the times he managed it, the times he was probably happy, even if he didn't tell us. I return to the chapbooks. My father, who was flesh and not glass, who was living matter and not iron, left proof of this fact in poems that don't announce to whom they're addressed. I reject sleep's promises to read him loving and laughing:

A mermaid surprised
It's noon and we're asleep.
Alicia removed the travel hammock from its case.
We used hooks and anchors
to fix it to the wall.
For now, we're pretending
that it's not the end of the world,
that Veracruz, Playa del Carmen, Los Cabos, the bays
of Nayarit
still exist.
We wake up again.
Let's make love on this beach, Alicia proposes.
The hammock bucks prodigiously
in the oscillations of orgasm.
Suddenly, a crack and we fall to the floor.
Gone are the sea, the breeze off the sand,
and the gleam of a sun that does not cut the skin.
But Alicia, with her legs wrapped in the hammock,
looks again like a surprised mermaid.

A capsule of love in the form of a poem. I hope it was Alicia, or whatever her name really was, who gave him Rosa Montero's book.

*

After immersing myself in his writing over the course of a few cloudy mornings, I grow bored of grief and want a distraction. I take another book off the shelf: a compilation of essays by Susan Sontag, underlined by my father. In the first essay, "An Argument About Beauty," the philosopher talks about how the idea of beauty has lost status over the course of a century defined by challenging hierarchies (itself being always a mark of value) and about the attempts to replace it with "the interesting." The word "interesting," however, has been emptied of meaning. Sontag's essay led me to a short video that has stayed in my head ever since I watched it a few years ago. In it, Slavoj Žižek asks, "Why Be Happy When You Could Be Interesting?" and points out how prolific suffering can be, especially compared to the paralysis occasioned by happiness. When we aspire to create, we are willing to suffer. This is a common notion among artists, as is its counterpart: happiness makes you stupid. Suffering is often celebrated far more than is healthy. Just as there is an aesthetic glorification of ugliness, which is often simply called being "interesting," there is also a glorification of sadness as a miracle cure for stupidity.

How many artists have bought into the idea that we can only create from that place? In *The Promise of Happiness*, Sara Ahmed criticizes the Anglo culture of self-help but says we shouldn't aspire to sadness because happiness is still ours to reclaim.

I think my father was so attached to the idea of the

interesting, unhappy, underappreciated man that he imbued the figure of The Great Loser with it. I also think about how I've walked the same line many times. The thing is, it's a tempting path—far from only putting you at a disadvantage, it offers real benefits. Maybe that's why so many people turn to the premise Yourcenar wrote for Alexis that I quoted earlier: "It is hard not to believe oneself superior when one is suffering." In the end, this too is a question of how we narrate ourselves.

You can bet my father suffered at the end, but—contrary to the myth—that suffering didn't help him create. Which seems central to the loss of desire. If life is a desire and not a meaning, then the road ahead must remain vital. In order to desire, we must aspire to something. As he left my book presentation two weeks before he died, my father wondered what would have happened if he had dedicated his energy to promoting his own work, rather than other people's. That retrospective question marks the absence of a horizon: there is no way to change this because there are no more books to promote. Everything that could have happened is already in the past.

*

Today I'm writing from the ruins. The certainty that I would find in words a solid meaning to ground me vanished in a night of cyclical insomnia, of looking at the clock every hour. It's three in the morning and, resigned to my sleeplessness, I pick up Rosa Montero's book:

With a death like that, like Pierre's; with a diagnosis like that, like Pablo's, the world crumbles. And, from the ruins, you obsess about the moment just before the quake, turning it over and over in your mind. If only I had known! you say. But no, you didn't know.

It does crumble, yes. How strange to think that in my father's final years, I was less afraid of his death than I was of his life. It never occurred to me to wonder what his death would mean to me, to my family or his friends. A little while before it happened, though, I remember telling a friend on our way back from a book festival that I thought it would probably happen soon. I don't remember what I felt when I said it. And sometimes I think I've been lying to myself all this time: I thought more about the pain of his existence and how he was wasting away because of the problems with his heart (in both senses) than about my fear of his approaching death. I was too afraid to admit that it was real.

*

The Ridiculous Idea of Never Seeing You Again is a monument to creativity as a weapon in the battle against sadness, against it becoming chronic. Our narratives are so important, on paper and off, and I still have so many questions about how I want to tell this story. Or, rather, how I want to tell my story, beyond my relationship with my father. The scrawl I am must be passed through other words.

EIGHTH: MAY GOD BLAST ANYONE WHO WRITES A BIOGRAPHY OF ME

Jardines de Kensington, Rodrigo Fresán, Literatura Mondadori, 2003. Net contents: an insane novel about the writer J. M. Barrie, among many other things.

"The writer as intermediary, as spirit guide, as elucidator of how books are the ghosts of living writers, and dead writers are the ghosts of books."

As if to compensate for having just written about a book my father surely didn't read, I pick up this volume entirely on purpose. Now that I know his library better, it's become clear that he has favourite writers. Rodrigo Fresán stands out with seven titles. Maybe there had been even more, and now they're gathering dust on their own shelf in some used bookstore. Maybe. Of the titles I do have, Alfonso informs me that *Kensington Gardens* was his favourite, but I could have guessed that based on the extensive underlining and how many page numbers have a blue box around them.

*

Half biography-on-steroids of J. M. Barrie, the diminutive author of *Peter Pan*, and half story of the madness of a children's book writer named Peter Hook, who also happens to be our illustrious narrator, one of the main themes of *Kensington Gardens* is the desire never to grow up, the fetish of eternal childhood, but always in connection with the end of a life. How strange that Fresán's book should have such a similar soul to the beginning of this one: a seemingly counterintuitive relationship between childhood and death. "We live, Keiko Kai, between two imaginary countries: that of the children we were and the dead we'll become," the narrator tells young Keiko Kai, the real or imaginary interlocutor he's holding prisoner in his London mansion.

In the beginning was childhood and in the end was his death. This book is only a continuation.

The dead end up as the fictions of those who survive them, who submit them to this indecent process of excision, addition and correction in the same way we all—exactly at the halfway mark—end up rewriting that other spectral realm: our childhood.

How strange that we need to return to childhood in order to talk about death.

*

To this day, *Kensington Gardens* is one of the grimmest books I've ever read. Like Barrie himself, who had close encounters with death starting when he was a little boy and his older brother died in an accident. His dark sense of humour is a clear example of the pain a person can hold inside them, and also of how art can shape that pain into something sublime, etc. without necessarily curing the emptiness at its centre.

Barrie famously said, "May God blast anyone who writes a biography of me." He had plenty of good reasons to fear such a thing. As do we all.

*

What fun it is to read about such extravagant characters. What a delight to follow their stories and their lysergic, homicidal, musical and literary adventures. What torture it would be to know them off the page. The paradox of what we love on paper but hate in life. Leafing through these gardens, I think about our need to distance ourselves from characters like these, as if we didn't all have their magic—sometimes malicious, sometimes benevolent—inside us, even if just a little bit. Characters who are free and brilliant, but also selfish and individualistic. Locked in an eternal emotional adolescence, with the hunger for the lightness of a child and an adult's capacity for harm. The characters they are, the characters we are. How would an author write us on any given day, depending on her mood, her resentments and her prejudices?

*

C. S. Lewis is the most important writer of my childhood. *The Chronicles of Narnia* put me on a collision course with the entire range of human emotion; the books were a rich display of what literature can do when it creates characters and worlds you want to inhabit despite freezing temperatures, dangers and betrayals. Praise be to the white witches and brave princes on the other side of the wardrobe. The seven illustrated books were some of the first I read on my own, and when I finished the last one—incredulous, disappointed at having reached the end and distraught over losing my little English friends—I asked my father, in vain, to write an eighth volume. Come to think of it, my terror of reaching the end of things, the fear that keeps me from reading the final pages of almost any book or watching the last episode in most series, probably comes from the loss of Narnia. Psychoanalytic interpretations welcome.

    C. S. Lewis wrote many Christian texts, fictions and otherwise, which meant that his work ceased to interest the adult version of me. Until now. I am reunited with the author of my childhood satyrs in the most unexpected place. Lewis wrote *A*

Grief Observed when his wife, the poet Helen Joy Davidman died of bone cancer just a few years after they were wed. The book's Wikipedia page offers a useful reminder: that the indefinite article in the title is meant to indicate that this is not an essay on pain, but rather one man's experience of losing his wife and his mourning as the path toward an encounter with his God. Lewis did not aspire to write a universal treatise; he wanted to portray his grief, which changed from moment to moment. The vitality of his reflections and the heart with which he submerges himself in his pain and questioning of God have made this one of my favourite books on mourning. Lewis asks himself to what extent it's possible to remember his dead wife:

> The image has the added disadvantage that it will do whatever you want. It will smile or frown, be tender, gay, ribald, or argumentative just as your mood demands. It is a puppet of which you hold the strings. Not yet of course. The reality is still too fresh; genuine and wholly involuntary memories can still, thank God, at any moment rush in and tear the strings out of my hands. But the fatal obedience of the image, its insipid dependence on me, is bound to increase.

Our dead are our puppets. My father is my puppet in this story. When I talk about him, I'm talking only about us. Lewis says that because he writes while his pain is so fresh, his heartfelt portrait is still able to transmit the reality of its subject. As a child of my time, I doubt this very much. If anything, I think that time tempers emotion and allows for a more rational portrait, if not necessarily a more faithful one. If that were the goal, it would be better to talk to many different people and build, testimony upon testimony, the prism of what the deceased was to others.

With all this in mind, I wonder still what I can say about my father that would mean something about him and not about me. Maybe what he was to me is also him, because we are how we shape our surroundings. As Joyce Carol Oates observes in *A Widow's Story*, "Our great American philosopher William James has said—*We have as many personalities as there are people who know us. To which I would add We have no personalities unless there are people who know us. Unless there are people we hope to convince that we deserve to exist.*"

The second response is far more relevant: my goal is not a faithful portrait but rather the fragile truths of literature.

*

My goal is not a faithful portrait, but that does not absolve me of the tremendous injustice of narrating someone's life who can't say anything at all about the matter. Not even the most grandiloquent ode is exempt from disagreements between author and subject.

I wonder what my father would think about my writing a book about him after his death. Would he be excited? Would he feel exposed? Would he be capable of asking his daughter to pen his official biography like José Donoso did? I do know this: to stick a band around the cover of this book crooning that it's a history of his life would be a total scam.

In *Lives Other Than My Own*, Jorge Volpi reports on a few of the ethical problems surrounding autofiction, memoir or whatever you want to call it. Henry Miller's disturbing portrait of his wife June in *Tropic of Cancer* is an extreme case, but Volpi points out that anyone who writes—whether they're young, old, famous or not—and has written about someone close to them has received some kind of reprimand, including him: "Because of a few paragraphs in a little book, my mother got angry and my brother didn't speak to me for a while." A friend of mine also met with her mother's displeasure when she wrote about her experience of her difficult divorce. She didn't paint her mother in a bad light at all, but it was enough of an affront that she had captured her private life on paper in view of so many, or so few.

Sergio Loo tells a similar story in *Operation on a Malignant Body*, his last book before cancer took his life:

> I've turned Cecilia's life into a nineteenth-century novel with thirty-seven chapters. As word of the novel has spread from mouth to mouth, with positive results, several favourable reviews have appeared. The sales, good. Soon the first edition will be sold out. Meanwhile Cecilia, increasingly pale, has turned into paper, a comic book page. Readers underline episodes from her life, and she feels stigmatised, buries the point of her pencil inside the sores. She can't stand up. She doesn't bleed. She's becoming famous, two-dimensional, public. She disappears.

Public, two-dimensional, her life turned into gossip. In the face of those cutting descriptions, it seems best to write only science fiction and leave flesh and bones in peace.

*

What a burden it must be to imagine your daughter offering a detailed account of every single time you hurt her, like the time you wrote the wrong month on her birthday party invitation and no one went. Not that you didn't feel bad enough when you saw her in her poufy floral dress waiting with tears in her eyes for her friends—who, of course, never arrived.

I guess this is one of the fears at the top of my list when I think about not having progeny. Not writing the date of a celebration wrong (impossible, after that trauma), but rather being at least partially responsible for someone else's suffering. I realise this logic is fuzzy because it leaves two things out: first, that this is true with or without descendants because no one is an island and pain is an inevitable part of life. Second, and more importantly, because it's not only pain we cause, but also—and especially—joy.

*

For now, I search the pages of others for answers to the question that is my father. What does "Life is a desire, not a meaning" mean, exactly? Perhaps, if life is a desire, then it makes sense to abandon it when one can no longer desire anything. After all, if there's no meaning, it's only held together by that initial impulse. Must one desire life in order to continue living? In Fresán's book, suicide is a constant presence. Its brutal beginning is a one-way flight onto the rails of the London tube taken by Peter Llewelyn Davies, one of the five brothers who inspired Barrie to write *Peter Pan*, first for the stage and then as a book. The eternal child, now an adult, flies from the rails into nothingness, cut up inside from the brutality he witnessed in World War I, where he fought and may indeed have died without losing his life. Later, Charles Frohman, theatre empresario and only adult friend to Barrie, becomes a sacrificial lamb in the sinking of the *Lusitania*, on which he is returning from America:

According to a surviving witness, Charles Frohman gives up his spot [on a lifeboat] and makes his goodbyes, saying: 'Why fear death? It is the greatest adventure in life.' Charles Frohman surrenders to death without the slightest resistance; with suspicious tranquillity, in my opinion. It's as if the theatre empresario were exploiting the epic advantages of the catastrophe to smuggle in a suicidal tourist as a stowaway, committing the perfect suicide; no one can reproach him for it because there's no bullet or rope or poison or final note explaining the inexplicable and asking that no one and nothing be blamed.

Suicide is the most lamented way to abandon this cruel world. When Peter—the other Peter, the Llewelyn Davies—takes his leap, the narrator imagines him thinking: "I'm so sorry to have to go so abruptly, so rudely, good night, God save the Queen and God have mercy on my soul and forgive me, forgive me, forgive me." I don't think he needed to apologise for lifting his broken wings and flying into that sea of steel. I realise this is an unpopular opinion.

After the death of his friend, Barrie begins to assert that Frohman should instead have exclaimed, "To die will be an awfully big adventure!" A phrase he puts in the mouth of Peter Pan on Marooners' Rock as the tide rises around him, though not during the Christmas performances of the play in 1915, when Barrie cut the scene to reduce production costs and because the line seemed a bit dark at a moment when dying was less an adventure than a part of everyday life.

*

That damned deathly smile he took with him to the grave. The overdose of sleeping pills I always thought was accidental. This investigation has led me to believe more and more that the peaceful expression on his face and the presence of that precise book on his stomach were no accident. Because "life is a desire, not a meaning," but it's also true that "to die will be an awfully big adventure." I'm not saying my father died by his own hand. I can't prove it. But I can't prove the opposite, either. In any case, God *don't* save the Queen but do have mercy on my father's soul. After all, the man was no atheist.

*

An almost childish idea runs through my mind as I read Fresán. I wish I could have talked with my father about this incredible story written in so many layers of truth and lies. I can see why this was one of his favourite books. I read further and am surprised by a parallel: Peter, the narrator, is reading the favourite book of his own father, who also, perhaps, died by suicide (which would make him a murderer, as well, because it would have meant that he intentionally sank a ship with other people aboard). The book—surprise, surprise—is *Peter Pan*. He analyses two paragraphs underlined in the book and understands something about his father. This passage was underlined by mine:

> The character is the past.
> The character is the way you relate to the past, how
> you ignore it and how you obey it.
> The way, for example, my father thought about yesterday, and the way I think about it.

Bibliomancy and psychoanalysis on the page since the beginning of time. Peter Hook's father never wanted to become a man. J. M. Barrie hated the idea of being an adult. I see a connection with Vila-Matas's bachelor machines. The Shandy secret society was, in a sense, a group of people who refused to grow up, to adhere to the conventions of the boring, serious, established adult world. In that sense, they also resembled my father. There's something wonderful in that, something profoundly revolutionary. The impulse to play at changing the world, which is the most serious game of all.

I go back to a time when his knees didn't send out shocks of pain and his hair was still nearly all brown. When the United States announced it would invade Iraq, my father got so angry he decided to do something. That was the beginning of what I remember as an incredibly long sheet of paper extending across the slate of the Zócalo. I run, like I always do, to Alfonso. "Who knows how Pascal got his hands on those huge, heavy rolls of newsprint for people to write their messages, fuck yous or whatever they thought about the gringo invasion of Iraq." For months, the Goliardos gathered signatures in the Zócalo and at El Chopo, book fairs and concerts. They never counted them, but instead of filling one roll of newsprint, they ended up filling five. At the end, they gave the rolls to Amnesty International Mexico at an event that included, naturally, a poetry reading. Moreover: the participants read anti-war poems that, to quote Alfonso, "Pascal forced us to write." We know the result of these efforts. It's not that this honourable act of opposition had any effect on United States foreign policy— nothing did. It's not that the war didn't happen. But at least there are always symbolic actions that challenge those in power. My father was an unrepentant idealist. Ultimately, poetry was the greatest of these spells; several poems scattered here and there translate this critical push into words:

Asymmetries

War is human notbeing, you say…
And asymmetrical war? I ask.
There's nothing like asymmetry
to reveal the inhumanity of the oppressor,
you reply.

It dawns on me that he really believed all that madness about
poetry being able to heal the world. There's no better definition of an idealist: rushing into the fray to fight injustice like
a modern-day Quixote. A line from e. e. cummings featured
in several Goliardos chapbooks rushes to mind: "but many a
thought shall die which was not born of dream." My father always added: "as long as we remember the words of Westphalen:
dreams are not a refuge but a weapon."
    All this, too, is the flesh and bone of my puppet.

*

I see myself in this sensibility, in this penchant for turning
literature into the only way to approach the world. I hope
dreaming remains a point of departure for me, that it never
becomes a painful stasis. There is no greater spell to ward off
depression than dreaming in order to fight, not in order to
escape.

*

His project of spreading literature everywhere, using every possible channel, whether these were respected or not, is one of
the most political things I have ever witnessed. Alfonso tells

me that he can't see all the good Goliardos did because he's still so blinded by its failure, but when I tell him that many people found a place for themselves as readers that didn't seem to exist anywhere else, a smile creeps across his face. "Yeah," he mutters, "maybe there's something to that." I also notice a subtle joy when he tells me about the things they did, whether minor or major. This, too, is the story he tells himself.

I repeat this and look down at the fanzine in my hands. It's called *A Sea of Words and Pleasures: A Literary Homage to H. Pascal* and it was published after his death by his students under an imprint called Legado Goliardos Ediciones—the legacy of Goliardos. At least they think it was all worth it. For these women, Goliardos was never a failure because unlike us they never projected the whole thing into the cosmos only to be rudely awakened on earth. The difference, as in so many things, has to do with expectations and where value is placed. And that's the part I should finish integrating into my own life story.

*

I close Fresán and take a big sip of green tea. After months and months of research in the company of these bookshelves, after pages and pages, I wonder: which of these words are my double, and which are my life? I certainly must have thought, wanted or even imagined a few of these things while others were actually happening. Memory, as we know, is a strange thing—not a closed archive but a reconstruction based on fragments held in different places of the brain. Every time we remember, we are actually imagining. Imagining, moreover, from the here and now, with the same cognitive strengths and weaknesses we bring to our life in the present.

I don't know if there's a way to be fair to a memory. I guess that's what people mean when they talk about relationships continuing even after someone is gone. Beyond who he was and what he did during his lifetime, when I talk to his ghost I'm talking both to my own pain and to his actions. It's a bio-logical process of subjective reconstitution. We construct what we can't grasp of our own experience and of what we observe in others by inventing meaning and building a world that didn't exist before we typed it out.

*

"The old bear was sometimes bad-tempered, but I never ques-tioned the size of his heart," writes Sofi Lara, one of his stu-dents, in *A Sea of Words and Pleasures*. I couldn't agree more.

Her words follow me as I become a wild horse among these dusty books. Today, during the dusting that happens once every few years, with rag in hand I am like someone spending unplanned hours with a photo album—I read ran-dom pages and tables of contents; I read beginnings, so many beginnings, and also a few endings, and between the dusty odour of cigarettes and paper I want to scream an ode to the memorious object that is the book and throw my e-reader in the trash, offering my eternal allegiance to this searing materi-ality over and against zeros and ones.

Now, their presence is not a burden but a joy; they are the warmth in my living room, the promise of a wise or tactile future in the past printed on the pages of books for everything: for crying, for comfort, for laughing, for imagination and ap-athy, for thoughts erratic and errant and also fair, for religions and nonsense, for the chance moments of existence. Love and death. I suddenly become a person who reads not with a critic's eye but for pleasure; I don't want to think about the strings pulled to make the world go around, about the ill-fated intersections of our lives or the omnipresence of violence. I just want to exist inside these books—to use them, as some have said, as a lovely form of escapism.

I caress the bookshelves, rub them with a viscous substance meant to nourish the wood; the rag massages their patient inhabitants while I think about the great fortune they hold, grateful they're in the living room of my ephemeral apartment.

NINTH: WHO IS LOOKING AT WHOM FROM THE DEPTHS OF THE SKY

The plants move from one end of my house to the other. Blue, yellow, purple and terra cotta pots travel from one window to the next in search of sunlight. A stubborn infestation of mealybugs kills the weakest among them. My black cat chews the spider plant until it's reduced to stubs, then it grows back. The pothos hangs there, sometimes buoyant, sometimes limp from lack of water. The snake plants reproduce like there's no tomorrow and end up breaching their borders.

In other words, time passes. It passes in books and in the people who pass through here. For now, the bookshelves are the natural paint on that wall, and I have an injury that keeps me from feeling half my chest and part of my back. Who would have thought that the most unsettling injury I've had in my life would be one that numbed me completely rather than one that hurt. An injection every day for nine days to restore my chest's ability to feel pleasure and pain. Nine. Just like the nine days of praying the Rosary that offer those who survive the right to return to a different version of their daily existence. A rite of passage on the way to a new life.

Rhythm is one of the principal ways the human brain regulates itself. A baby who cries and is then rocked gently by her mother will continue to cry until she finds her own rhythm in the arms rocking her. Praying the Rosary to the rhythm of its beads has a very real effect on the person running their fingertips over the long necklace. Traditional rites of passage revel in cadence as a ritual of return.

I find my rhythm each time I run my fingertips over a keyboard. The letters appear on the screen and one by one they form patterns like dances of feeling. My writing routines are my Rosary, what I have is this ritual. In the name of the Father, the Son and the Holy Spirit; voices incanting in unison, bodies vibrating in a shared space during the novena. I, on the other hand, am accompanied solely by these books.

The months, which pass by the bunch—sweet cherries, bitter cherries—send me looking backwards in the hope of seeing differently. I stand and search the bookshelves for something to help me reconnect. My fingers explore their surface, looking for something undefined. Hands, do your work of divination. Tell me once and for all what you want.

*

Maybe to escape the reality that every day brings me closer to the end of these nine months, I choose a book that brought us together in life, as well.

La invención de la soledad, Paul Auster, Anagrama, 1994. Translated by María Eugenia Ciocchini. Net contents: two books about paternity in one.

"To begin with death. To work my way back to life, and then, finally, to return to death. Or else: the vanity of trying to say anything about anyone."

Paul Auster the essayist mourns with pen in hand. The memoir of his encounter with a ghost makes me return to the pages before this and add fragments throughout my novena. I toss it backward like a bottle on the high seas of this book, to find necessary spaces here and there. Ultimately, there's something meaningful in the fact that it comes from his library and will end up being used to talk about his death.

*

The question of why my father left it all behind, why he wasn't what he *should have* been, why he abandoned something that seemed so iron-clad, was a painful mystery for me. I kept hoping for a special alternative to the typical answer: depression, frustration, masculinity. Pain. But also: the barbaric world we inhabit.

Paul Auster, on the other hand, quickly discovers an answer he didn't know he needed. His father, with his steady and stoic, even somewhat grey, personality carried a brutal family history from when he was just a young boy: Auster's grandmother killed his grandfather, and his father suffered a childhood marked by social rejection, guilt and grief. Faced with this information, like the grain of sand that contains an entire universe, Auster understands everything. His father's hardness and apparent mediocrity were the fruit of a childhood wound so great it left him mute.

Perhaps it's the fault of stories like these, stories that offer spectacular answers to mundane questions, that we're always searching for something more. I've stopped searching for explanations. Now, above all else, I search for the courage to love.

*

"See you later, I'm just going to visit Mum," a man tells C. S. Lewis before visiting a grave. Lewis is horrified, but later understands: "A six-by-three-foot flowerbed had become Mum." That's how those who have lost someone keep a symbol of their time with us. A friend keeps a necklace; my grandmother, a sewing machine. I keep a few books and a t-shirt. We didn't bury my father. We didn't know what to do with his ashes, either. My brother and I tried to figure it out for a while, and the closest we got to an answer (though I soon realised the idea was completely bonkers) was to spread his ashes somewhere in the Centro Cultural José Martí.

What do you do with someone's ashes? The image of someone scattering them over the sea, however appealing it might sound to others, always reminds me of that scene in *The Big Lebowski* where Walter tosses Donnie's ashes over the coast but the wind carries them back and they end up all over the Dude's face. Plus, as far as I know, my father was more urban in his sensibilities.

Having discarded the traditional solutions of beach, forest and cultural centre, we left my father's ashes to gather dust in a corner. We don't look at them often; in fact, we kind of avoid them in an effort to strip them of all meaning, because it's hard to find eternal rest in an urn without any sort of ritual discourse. So many things become clear in retrospect, like the point of putting bones in a specific place or observing burial rites.

"A religious burial is not for the dead person, but for his immediate family and relatives, and so his beliefs matter little if those who survive prefer to have a certain kind of funeral for him," says Héctor Abad, but I wonder if my father wanted a religious burial, monthly mass, Rosaries and other things we didn't do. For a long time, I was convinced that my grandmother hated me because there had been no ritual at all, aside from the wake my uncle organised. I thought I could hear a reproach in her voice, grainy with sadness, just like when I didn't offer any remarks at his wake, but Alfonso gave a moving speech in the role of putative son.

My grandmother did go to church every month and anniversary. I'm sure she asked for a mass to be dedicated to my father. Now I think it might have been a bit cruel not to have organised something to comfort her, even if it went against our own beliefs. Sometimes I think she needs a grave to return to, a place to "visit her son."

I think about her because it's easier than thinking about my brother or me. Were we affected somehow by the absence of a funeral mass? Of the Rosaries we didn't pray? Or even the neo-pagan ritual we couldn't manage to invent? A wake one afternoon and then a cremation; an urn with ashes that I haven't even seen because it ended up at my mother's house, abandoned there by my brother. That was and is all. My ritual is this book. I don't know about my brother's.

*

Paul Auster says that there are no surprise endings in a book about mourning. I would add that, even if the ending offers no surprise, everything that comes before is a series of surprises for the person writing. This form of intimate research is like nothing else. It's a séance during which you revive in literature the things life forced you to bury. The question is from where to invoke the spirit. Auster does it from the present tense, as he empties a house and names a living ghost.

His father. "Even before his death he had been absent, and long ago the people closest to him had learned to accept this absence, to treat it as the fundamental quality of his being." He also says, elsewhere: "For fifteen years he had lived alone. Doggedly, opaquely, as if immune to the world." I think about how much that resembles my feelings about how my father abandoned the world. Maybe Auster decided to write the second part of his book, in which he focuses on his own role as father, because the first was so harsh. As a daughter who is only a daughter, I've had to ponder my emotions from a different angle.

*

A phrase echoes in me. "To begin with death. To work my way back to life, and then, finally, to return to death." With all this weight I've been carrying, all these pages trying to decipher a life, there's nothing I'd rather do right now than return to death. My mind returns to the final image of my father in his bed with a book about writing poetry open on his belly. A peaceful expression on his face—happy, even. And I decide, as I did then, to join him in that feeling.

*

Maybe this is why I return to a memory that usually ushers in The Pain, but which feels luminous today. The year before he died, I had an unusual impulse: I invited him to a restaurant for his birthday. I was surprised that he agreed to eat at a German place called Nibelungengarten near my apartment, since he so rarely left his neighbourhood. At the appointed hour, I waited for him outside the restaurant. I paced back and forth, looking up and down the block while he insisted that he was there waiting for me. Just as I was beginning to question my eyesight and my sanity, we figured out what was going on. He was waiting for me there, which is to say in front of his building, and I was already here, where we were supposed to meet. We were in different spaces trying to achieve the same end, which required us to be in the same place. It was hopeless. My first (and last) attempt to invite him out ended before it began. Now, the simple fact of having tried after so many years of distance means something to me. There's so much truth in that apparently hollow phrase: you don't get to choose when someone dies. I had no way of knowing that would be his last birthday. The attempt was valuable in its own right; the attempt was love. Again: so much depends on how you narrate something, on the lens through which you view an event.

*

Even the idea that his death was voluntary, which has been fluttering around inside me for months, has a new tint to it. I begin to wonder if his way of living, walled in by books without ever getting rid of any of them, might have come from the knowledge that it was all he could leave me. Maybe my involuntary inheritance, as I've been describing the volumes currently collecting dust in my apartment, wasn't so involuntary, after all. Maybe he knew it was the most generous gift he could give me, more generous even than money or property (both of which were out of his reach, anyway). It's true that in this sea of questions, there were always the many answers found in those books—both in the ideas they contained, and in the sheer materiality of them.

I grab one of the many duplicate volumes from among his ample collection of poetry published by Lumen. It's by Cristina Peri-Rossi, and a page in it is marked.

Dedication II
Literature separated us: everything I learned about
you
I learned in books,
and what was missing
I gave it words.

Writing is a vital impulse: we go on living, somehow, as long as we keep creating. I go on living while I write him. And so, even though my father stopped writing almost entirely two years before his death, there were still wellspring moments amid all that drought. For example: a poem he wrote to the Topos, a brave group of rescue workers who called themselves moles and dug into the ruins of Mexico City after it was torn apart by an earthquake in 2017, at the same time he was organising a drive with his students to bring food to those helping out in the fallen buildings in Lindavista, where he lived. Never a more literal moment for that line from e. e. cummings he liked so much: "though wish and world go down, one poem yet shall swim."

Later, lost in the desert of writing, my father managed to pen his final oasis: the poem "Proof of Existence," which announces the end two months before his death. It's about personal history and the body, this vessel that holds us together and becomes so present in illness.

> And this bear body of mine
> with its tremendous,
> irresponsible hospitality
> and its soul, clean and true.

"Suicide by carbohydrates and cigarettes," says Alfonso, and I counter: "Suicide by neglect of the body in general." When I pierced my navel for the first time, my father looked at me with disappointment in his eyes. "Your body is a temple and you've profaned it," he said. I've never been one for sacred things or being given orders, so his words bounced right off me. Now I find myself thinking about the image, which he so energetically embraced, of the body as a temple of pleasure. Eating, fucking and smoking. Especially the former. There are stories that have nearly passed into the realm of legend about how Pascal could drive the owner of a little spot in Lindavista crazy over their all-you-can-eat-taco deal. There are stories, so many stories, about the greasy feasts he hosted. I witnessed the bags of chilli-dusted candies he bought and the number of cookies he was able to eat. His love for chorizo almost qualified as an ode. Kilos of cheese that were nearly a poem themselves when they began sizzling in his pan. His German sausage and beer soups, the faithful accompaniment to his Pascalised shandies. The moment he dipped a spoon into a bubbling stew to see if the salt and fat were right, and then shook his mullet while a resounding *mmmmmh* came out of him. I witnessed, in other words, the tremendous, irresponsible hospitality of his bear body.

The poem goes on to talk about what I understand as the loss of desire, that death of a horizon:

Luck hasn't changed,
it is seen from afar
or from too close:
the fate is the same.
Looking into oneself
as if into a piercing pit.
But who is looking at whom
from the depths of the sky?

His fate did, in fact, seem to be written in stone. Seriously ill, on the outs with almost everyone, unemployed, asking for money left and right, even from me. Unable to write. Debts, back rent. His work, visible to only a few; certainly not what he would have wanted. In his darkest moments, that piercing pit must have knocked the air out of him. The poem continues with lines that are either more brutal or more platonic, depending:

> There is no possible legacy:
> this bear body
> has only had
> this intangible soul.

I've asked myself time and again what he's trying to say with this goodbye. The desperation of thinking your life's work is meaningless? The artist dreams of being transcendent. The reality is that they rarely achieve this aim. On which side of the scales did he think he was sitting? Here, again, our guiding phrase: life is a desire, not a meaning. I don't see desire or meaning in these lines anymore.

*

Legacy comes from the Latin *lego*, which means, among other things, to read. I'm reading you now, even if I wasn't able to read the account of your existence back then.

*

And then life breaks through writing's solipsism. A post on social media by his former student Sofi Lara shakes me out of the piercing pit into which I, too, am beginning to fall.

213

Dear H. Pascal,

It's almost your birthday. They're going to publish a children's story of mine. I put more into it than ever before and I did it. This achievement, however small, is dedicated to you. I wish I could have brought a copy to the Martí for you.

I miss you lots. Thank you.

The most needed embrace. We are also what we've been to others.

*

My father died on the second of July. Two Sundays earlier, it had been Father's Day. I was about to go on vacation with my partner. He asked me if we were going to get together that day and I said no, I had too much work to finish before my trip. But my brother could, of course. I let him fulfil all our filial duties, again. The way I saw it, him going with his partner and kid to see my father definitely covered the space I wasn't going to occupy. If we were counting chairs, we'd even come out one ahead.

The following week, he went to stay at my uncle's house in Hidalgo.

My mother told me that my father had argued with a relative, who, in the middle of a one-sided dispute (my father was calm), screamed at him that he was a miserable pig. The insult struck a nerve, so much so that a few days later he told my mother over the phone that, sure, he was overweight and all, but he wasn't miserable. Sometimes I decide to believe him. Because towards the end of his life he went to my uncle's house often and was happy there with my grandmother; because the cook, Maribel, says he was always cracking her up and that he enjoyed every bite of his meals; because his landlady told us that a few weeks before he died, even with all the back rent he owed, he invited her out for quesadillas at the stand on the corner and they both smiled the whole time. She liked him so much she didn't even ask us to pay his debt. A Pascalised shandy for her.

And because of the final lines from "Proof of Existence," which talk about something more than despair:

> But there is nothing
> I have managed
> without the two together,
> stillness and lives,
> feelings and stories,
> and even loves that were,
> intemperate temples,
> reconstructed ruins;
> the expansive joy
> of two beautiful children:
> vehement intelligence,
> clouds brimming…
> An implacable saint of
> a mother, screaming and powerful,
> and siblings blessed
> by eccentric gods;
> so many poems
> that might be novels,
> a dozen stories
> with a touch of poetry;
> Zócalos filling
> with shadows and song,
> with rebellious throngs,

lives, transmutations;
women in streetcars,
the seduction and the fall,
blood among ideas
and poem kisses;
the physical excitement
of thinking minds,
spirits of their time:
students and teacher.
A soul that speaks in tongues
and wanders serene,
a monolingual body
rightfully restless,
and the blood that unites,
and the time that distracts
this bear body,
this fleeing soul…

If his soul is already fleeing, at least the poem is able to find the meaning of existence in the moments he lived. It swims. And I think that if he stopped smoking, even if only for a few weeks, then he didn't want to die. Not all the time, at least. That if he told me, less than a month before, that the road back to health was slow and difficult, then he still hoped to travel it. That if he died with that tranquil look on his face and that book on his belly, then somewhere inside he must have been at peace. That maybe he wasn't writing, but he was reading, and he was still chasing immortality in the cult of knowledge. That he loved being with his grandson and would have wanted to see him grow up. That he was really proud of me and my brother.

I think about his face, red from his illness, at my book presentation; about him watching me sign a copy for one of his students and the joy in his voice when he declared that I signed my books with nice handwriting, unlike his lifelong scrawl.

I think about all the love he gave me and all the love he gave to others, and I cry alone while writing a book that is a ritual intoned to the rhythm of my keyboard. Maybe I feel it so deeply because I know this novena is almost at its end.

My father's hugs were a sweet mountain, a whisper of years of affection. He shared his knowledge not as a string of facts but as offerings of tenderness and enthusiasm. He cooked pure love into each delicious, dilettante dish bubbling on his stovetop.

Indirectly and despite everything, he managed to find ways to be with me. Across various forms of distance, we kept meeting outside the Eugenia metro station year after year, and he kept giving me those curious parcels of his—a book, packets of tuna and two hundred pesos—that held all the feelings he couldn't express. And I would receive them without breaking our pact of silence. For years, we each managed to keep an arm extended just enough that the tips of our fingers always touched.

His books, the most symbolic object of all, managed to survive even his death. The gift he gave everyone, whether they wanted it or not, so he could repeat these quiet mantras: this is who I am and I care about you. I am a man who gives books to people who don't read. I am a man who has just enough money to give these increasingly random objects. This is who I am, and I care about you deeply.

I want to invent a new tradition, like the bridal ritual of wearing something old, something new, something borrowed and something blue. Or the one about taking an empty suitcase for a walk on New Year's Eve while wearing red underwear. It will go like this: you give someone a book, a packet of tuna and two hundred pesos—each object the symbol of a loving wish you hold for their recipient. I suggest repeating this once a year or whenever you want to strengthen your bond with someone, to pamper them with a gift that says: I care about you deeply and wish you the very best. I think of you often. And even: I love you.

Bibliography of translated works

Abad Faciolince, Héctor. *Oblivion*, trans. Anne McLean and Rosalind Harvey. Farrar, Straus and Giroux, 2012.

Calderón de la Barca, Pedro. *Life is a Dream*, trans. Stanley Applebaum. Dover Thrift Editions, 2002.

Calvino, Italo. *Cosmicomics*, trans. William Weaver. Mariner Books, 1976.

Fresán, Rodrigo. *Kensington Gardens*, trans. Natasha Wimmer. Faber, 2005.

Loo, Sergio. *Operation On a Malignant Body*, trans. Will Stockton. Kin(d)* Texts & Projects, 2019.

Peri Rossi, Cristina. *Evohé: erotic poems*, trans. Diana P. Decker. Azul Editions, 1994.

Vallejo, Irene. *Papyrus*, trans. Charlotte Whittle. Knopf, 2022.

Vila-Matas, Enrique. *A Brief History of Portable Literature*, trans. Anne McLean and Thomas Bunstead. New Directions, 2015.

Vila-Matas, Enrique. *Montano's Malady*, trans. Jonathan Dunne. New Directions, 2007.

Villaurrutia, Xavier. *Nostalgia for Death*, trans. Eliot Weinberger. Copper Canyon Press, 1993.

THANK YOU

To Kyzza Terrazas, Diego Rabasa, Gabriela Jauregui, Emiliano Monge and Paula Canal. I couldn't have finished this book without your comments, care and encouragement. Especially Kyzza, who read these pages so many times he probably has nightmares about gothic metal concerts in the Zócalo. To Libia Brenda Castro and Alfonso Franco for being readers and informants. Without you, I wouldn't have been able to reconstruct an important part of my father's complexity. To all the people who wrote to me or shared anecdotes. I didn't include all of them, but they are all part of this book. To Elisa Díaz Castelo and César Tejeda for commenting on snippets of this book when it was still learning to crawl. To my loving and beloved little writing group: Alfredo Bojórquez, Sujaila Miranda, Irasema Fernández, Danush Montaño, Berenice Andrade. To Mariano del Cueto for holding me together in the months after the event. To Mariano, Diego Rodríguez Landeros and Danush for helping me decide which books to save. To Alfonso, Mireli Alcántara (Mili), Marko González and Margarita Pacheco for being there the day we emptied my father's apartment. To Pierre Herrera and Olivia Teroba for unpacking the books in my apartment when I couldn't even look at them. To the women of Goliardos for being at his side. To Andrea Montejo and Paula again, for accompanying me and offering advice through fair weather and foul. To my mother, Angélica, and Juan, my brother, for all the obvious reasons and more. To my uncles, my aunt and grandma García-Junco for being part of this story. To everyone who was at my side throughout the endless process of mourning that is the death of a father.

I wrote a first draft of this book with a grant from the Young Creators programme (2020-2021) under the tutelage of Minerva Anguiano, Gonzalo Lizardo and Cuauhtémoc Peña, accompanied by Erik Alonso, María José Amaral, Lilia Ávalos, Diego Casas Fernández, Adrián Chávez, Jesús Estrada Milán, Mariana Orantes and Sofía Saravia. Thank you for your comments and for pushing me to keep writing.

Aura García-Junco, born and based in Mexico City, is the au-thor of three novels and one longform essay. She also works as a screenwriter, critic, columnist and occasional translator. She studied Classical Literature at the Universidad Nacional Autónoma de México and was a scholar at the Foundation for Mexican Letters (2016) and the FONCA Young Creators Programme (2014, 2017 and 2021). In 2021, she was select-ed by *Granta* as one of the 25 Best Young Spanish-Language Novelists. *May God Blast the Woman Who Writes About Me* is the first of her novels to be translated into English, with an-other, *Sea of Stone*, set to be published in 2025.

Heather Cleary is a translator and writer based in New York and Mexico City. Her writing has appeared in Two Lines, Lit Hub and Words Without Borders, among other publications. In 2021, she co-edited *McSweeney's 65: Plundered* with Valeria Luiselli and, in 2022, her book, *The Translator's Visibility: Scenes from Contemporary Latin American Fiction*, was published by Bloomsbury. Her translations have won and been nominat-ed for several of the most prestigious awards and grants for works in translation. She has served on the jury of the National Book Award in Translation, the Queen Sofia Spanish Institute Translation Award, the Best Translated Book Award and the PEN Translation Award. She holds a PhD in Latin American and Iberian Cultures from Columbia University and teaches at Sarah Lawrence College.